BOUND BY MYSTERY

BEACH BOUND BOOKS AND BEANS MYSTERIES
BOOK 3

CHRISTY BARRITT

River Heights

CHAPTER
ONE

TALI FROWNED as she stared at the emergency alert message on her phone.

"I'm so sorry, but it looks like you're going to be stuck here," she muttered to the ladies around her. "The ferry just shut down for the rest of the day because of the storm."

A nor'easter seemed to have whipped up out of nowhere. It hadn't been on any of the forecasts Tali had seen. Yet now it tormented them with driving rain, strong winds, and elevated sea levels.

This was bad news for the three bookstore owners from neighboring islands who'd come to visit her.

"I suppose that's always the risk of visiting an island with no bridges." Gia Manning frowned as they stood just inside the door leading from Tali's bookstore/coffeehouse out to the boardwalk.

The thirty-something woman loved bright red lipstick and was Italian, about fifty pounds over-weight, and gregarious—not the typical bookworm type at all. But she could talk up a book with the best of them. If you wanted an influencer, she was your woman.

"I can stay with my cousin here on the island," Alice Briggs said. "I'll just leave first thing in the morning. It's no problem."

Fifty-five-year-old Alice owned a bookstore on Hatteras Island. The petite, mousy brunette seemed quiet—until you got to know her. Then she was as friendly as a cozy pair of socks on a cold winter day.

"And I can stay with my friend Wanda," Gia said. "If she heard I came to the island and didn't stop by to see her, I would be in hot water anyway. It's all fine."

Thunder cracked overhead at her words.

As the storm continued to strengthen, Tali couldn't wait to get upstairs to her apartment to curl up with a blanket and watch the storm raging outside over the ocean.

It was one of her favorite things to do—especially when her dog, Sugar—a Westie—was by her side.

Tali turned to Donna Winters, who owned a book-store on Hatteras.

Donna, in her early sixties, had completely gray

hair and a reserved demeanor that almost made her seem as if she had no personality at all. From what Tali had heard, Donna had a bit of a paranoid streak, and when her anxiety kicked in, everyone around her felt it. She read so many crime novels that she saw danger around every corner and the police no longer came right away when she called. That was the rumor, at least.

Of the three, Donna was Tali's least favorite—though she hoped that didn't show.

"Any of you would be welcome to stay here, of course." Tali had an extra bedroom and two couches.

"If you don't mind, I'm going to take you up on the offer." Donna frowned as if she'd rather pluck off her eyebrows than make someone go out of their way for her. "But I hate to impose."

"Don't apologize," Tali murmured. "I hate that you're all stuck here on the island. I know you have other things to do."

"We've lived in this area longer than you, so we should've known better." Gia shrugged. "It's just that when we got caught up talking about that new C.J. Box book, we didn't hear the wind picking up."

After a few more minutes of conversation, Alice and Gia hurried toward their cars.

When they disappeared from sight, Donna turned

to Tali. "I'm rather tired. Is it okay if I turn in for the evening?"

Tali was more than happy to oblige. She was ready for some time alone.

"Of course. Let's get upstairs."

The woman followed her upstairs, where Tali's apartment was located. Tali showed her where to find the bathroom and toiletries and got her settled in the spare bedroom.

"Thank you again for letting me stay here." Donna nodded, her face expressionless—not friendly or hostile. Just kind of . . . vanilla.

"Of course. It's no problem."

Before Tali left the room, Donna took something from her pocket and slipped it into Tali's hand. She leaned close as if she had a secret. "Don't open this now. Wait until tomorrow."

Tali glanced down at the letter-sized envelope in her hands. "What is it?"

"You'll see." Donna's gaze remained on Tali another moment as if she were silently trying to communicate.

But Tali had no idea *what* she was trying to communicate or why she wouldn't just come right out and say it.

The woman was becoming more peculiar by the moment.

Donna closed the door to the spare bedroom, eliminating any further conversation.

Tali stood there a moment and stared at the envelope with its rumpled edges.

It was lightweight, with nothing written on the outside of it.

What could be inside? Should she honor Donna's wish and not open it now?

She was entirely too impatient to wait too long.

Could she wait until morning?

Tali pressed her lips together.

Of *course*, she could wait.

She was an adult. She could do this.

But she would be thinking about it all night.

———

Tali had thought about the letter all night.

As soon as she'd awoken—and it was officially a new day—she sat up and grabbed it from her nightstand.

Her gaze skimmed her alarm clock as she did. The red numbers blinked.

Had the power gone out last night?

Apparently.

Her gaze went back to the envelope.

She still had no clue what it could contain or why Donna had acted so mysterious about it.

The storm still raged outside, thunder rattling the walls as she stared at the white envelope.

"Let's see what's inside this," she muttered to Sugar, who lay at her feet.

The dog stretched, wagged his tail, and then pranced toward her.

Waiting no longer, Tali ripped open the seal on the envelope and glanced inside.

She squinted.

A small scrap of paper with torn edges waited there.

Sitting on the edge of her bed, she pulled out the paper and studied it.

One side was blank. On the other, a single word was carefully handwritten in ink.

Calibrate.

"Calibrate?" she muttered to Sugar with a frown. "What sense does *that* make?"

None.

It wasn't like Donna was secretly a mechanic— and she didn't seem the type to be involved in technology.

So why would she write this word down and give it to Tali?

What else could the word calibrate refer to?

"This is strange," Tali muttered to Sugar.

The dog wagged his tail in response.

Tali stared at the paper another moment before shoving it back into the envelope. Then she put the envelope in her nightstand drawer.

She had company, which meant that she needed to get up. Donna would most likely want breakfast, and she'd *definitely* want coffee.

Tali showered, dressed in her favorite linen pants and a cream-colored knit top, then stepped into her Birkenstocks. She called it her "coastal grandma" look.

Tali was surprised when she stepped from her bedroom and saw everything was quiet in her apartment. She'd assumed her guest would be up already.

Maybe Donna liked to sleep in.

Tali whipped up some homemade banana nut muffins and stuck them in the oven. Soon, their scent would fill the place. Tali closed her eyes and sniffed as she imagined the sweet aroma.

She *loved* the smell of freshly baked treats mingling with coffee almost as much as she loved the scent of the ocean as it wafted through her windows on the autumn breeze.

October on the island was going to be magnificent. She was certain of it.

She needed to take Sugar outside, so she hurried downstairs.

But when she hit the bottom step and turned toward her shop, Tali stopped in her tracks.

Donna lay in the middle of Tali's beautiful, not yet completely renovated bookstore . . . a knife shoved into her back.

CHAPTER
TWO

MAC PULLED the hood of his slicker closer around his face as the wind and rain beat down on everything in sight.

According to forecasters, this weather wouldn't let up for several more days.

He'd parked in a public lot and headed toward Tali's place to check on her.

He was probably overstepping.

He'd soon find out.

It had been three weeks since the two of them had last spoken.

And what a wonderful evening they'd had the last time they were together.

They'd been at a beach party under the pier.

Lanterns and string lights had been strung between the huge pilings. Hammocks stretched on the outskirts of the place. Carter Denver, a local musician, played the guitar above them on the pier.

Tali had agreed to dance with Mac. So they'd swayed in each other's arms as the salty ocean breeze wafted about. Tali's sweet scent and the feel of her soft skin against his had done something to him.

Which was a shame since Mac knew the two of them could never be together.

He frowned at the thought and pulled his hood down lower to avoid the driving rain.

Tali hadn't lived on the island long, and this storm was a real doozy. Tide levels were high, which made the beach almost disappear as the water lapped close to the dunes and the boardwalk.

Plus, power on Lantern Beach had gone out for several hours last night—something not uncommon here on the isolated island. Now only about half of the island had their electricity back on.

He was just being neighborly by checking on her.

Right?

He reached the storefront for Beach Bound Books and Beans and paused a moment. Before he raised his hand to knock, he caught a glance of the store through the door's window and paused.

Tali was already downstairs. She stood frozen, staring at something and clutching Sugar with one hand and her heart with the other.

Instantly, his instincts went on alert. Being a police chief on the island for thirty years had honed that. He'd retired several years ago, but some things never left a person.

Investigative instinct was one of those.

He quickly knocked on the door.

As he did, Tali startled then glanced at him with wide, frightened eyes .

She rushed to the door, unlocked it, and threw it open. Her movements appeared frantic, and her voice trembled as she said, "Mac . . . I'm so glad you're here."

Those were the *exact* words Mac wanted to hear . . . but he was nearly certain the context was lacking. Sugar panted and whined in Tali's arms, only confirming that fact.

He bristled as he waited for bad news. "What's going on?"

With one hand still over her heart and the other clutching Sugar, she nodded to something in the distance. "Oh, Mac . . . it's Donna . . ."

Sensing her distress, he stepped inside the bookstore. As soon as he peered around the nearest bookshelf, he sucked in a breath.

A woman lay face down on the floor with a knife protruding from her back.

Mac rushed toward the woman and checked her

pulse.

There was none.

He glanced up at Tali, his years of experience kicking in. "Have you called the police yet?"

Tali appeared numb with shock as she stood there gawking.

"No . . . I just found her. She couldn't get off the island, so she stayed with me last night. Now she's . . ." Tali's voice faded as if she couldn't finish the sentence.

"Why don't you sit down?" Mac stood and led her to an upholstered blue chair in the corner before she collapsed. "Take a few deep breaths."

As soon as she was seated, he pulled out his phone and called the police for her. Police Chief Cassidy Chambers promised to be right out.

He put his phone away and stood in front of Tali, purposefully blocking her view of the woman.

"What was Donna's full name?" He needed to keep Tali distracted.

"Donna Winters. She owns a bookstore on Hatteras Island. She and two other bookstore owners came to visit me yesterday. They were trapped on the island by the storm and the ferry closing and . . ." Tali's voice drifted as her eyes clouded with memories.

"When was the last time you spoke to her?"

"Last night before I went to bed. She wanted to turn in early, but she seemed fine then." Her eyes widened. "Except . . ."

Mac bristled with apprehension. "Except what?"

Tali shook her head, almost too quickly. "Donna handed me an envelope before she went to bed and told me not to open it until today. So, of course, I did that first thing when I woke up. I couldn't wait any longer."

"What was inside?"

She rubbed her throat, her gaze still glazed with shock. "It was . . . a torn sheet of paper with a singular word handwritten across it. *Calibrate*."

He squinted. "Why would she give you something like that?"

Tali shrugged. "Your guess is as good as mine."

With his hands on his hips, Mac turned and studied the room. There were no signs of a struggle— just a dead body.

He turned back to Tali. "Have you touched anything?"

"Nothing except maybe the stair railing when I came down. My knees aren't exactly what they used to be." She let out a coarse chuckle that ended abruptly as she seemed to remember the situation. "As soon as I got down here, I saw Donna. That's when you showed up."

A bad feeling brewed inside him.

Why did trouble keep seeming to find Tali?

Mac wasn't sure.

He only knew that he'd be there to help her—if she'd let him.

———————

Police Chief Cassidy Chambers had shown up at Beach Bound Books and Beans to investigate the crime scene.

Unfortunately, this was becoming a monthly occurrence.

Tali wasn't sure why mystery seemed to keep following her. Sure, she might love reading mystery novels and watching *Dateline* specials. But that didn't mean she wanted to be involved with them in real life.

"We're going to need to check your security footage from the camera outside." Cassidy shifted as she stood near a floor-to-ceiling bookshelf inside Beach Bound Books and Beans.

"Of course." With trembling hands, Tali pulled up the app on her phone.

Mac had helped her install the system after danger kept appearing at her door.

The man had been a real lifesaver ever since she

came to the island. She hated to admit it because he was also the man who'd ruined her life many years ago—without even knowing it.

Without even knowing *her*.

Tali frowned as she stood near what would be her coffee counter once the shop opened. The bar-height serving area helped her keep her balance as she leaned on the butcher-block top.

She clicked on the security camera history and frowned.

Mac moved in closer—maybe too close. Close enough that Tali felt the warmth of his body. That she smelled his spicy cologne.

The memories of the last time they'd been together—when they'd danced beneath the pier—filled her mind.

That sweet moment was the last thing that she needed to think about. The moment had been too cozy.

In other words, it was off-limits.

She stared at her phone screen and shook her head. "The videos aren't here."

"What?" Mac held out his hand. "Do you mind?"

She thrust the phone into his hand, happy to be rid of this responsibility.

But after Mac looked at the screen for several minutes, he frowned also. "The power outage must've done something to the cameras. There's no feed from the last eight hours."

Cassidy peered around him and shook her head. "That's unfortunate."

Cassidy had two other officers with her who were checking the place for clues and fingerprints. They were going to find a lot of them, considering the number of people who'd been in and out of here recently.

It almost seemed like that included half the town.

Tali had a lot of contractors and even people from church come in to help her with some work she'd been doing. She'd also hosted a lady's tea for some other widows at her church. Then there was her book club and the bookstore owners who had visited.

It was going to be a lot to sort through. Tali thought, based solely on her experience as a mystery novel connoisseur, that none of those people—those fingerprints—would lead anywhere.

Doc Clemson, the medical examiner, was also here examining the body. He made jabbing motions with his fisted hand as if he were trying to determine the angle the blade had gone in while humming "Back Stabbers" by the O'Jays.

Mac had explained once that people in this line of work had to have a sense of humor. Otherwise, they'd take everything they saw and experienced home with them. Humor helped build emotional separation.

At first, their actions had seemed irreverent. But now Tali understood.

Tali kept her back toward Donna. She couldn't bear to see her colleague like that. It would take a long time to get the image of this dead body out of her mind.

"And you didn't hear anything last night?" Cassidy stepped closer as if trying to keep Tali's attention on her instead of the tragedy in her shop. "Or Sugar? Did he bark?"

Tali scooped her dog up and rubbed his head. "No, it's so strange. He usually lets me know if anything is amiss—even if it's just a bird or a squirrel outside the window. But he slept soundly beside me last night. He doesn't love thunderstorms, so he was under the covers. Maybe that threw him off or something."

She shrugged, unsure about the psychology of canines.

"Is there anything else you can tell me?" Cassidy locked her gaze with Tali's as if she meant business.

Tali had already given the police chief a recap of what had transpired last night, and she'd handed over the note with the word *calibrate*.

She stole one more glance over her shoulder, her

gaze stopping before it reached Donna's body. Instead, Tali studied the stack of books on the floor near where Donna lay. She'd seen them earlier and hadn't thought anything about them initially.

But now she realized they were out of place.

"Those books weren't there last night when I went to bed."

Cassidy narrowed her eyes as she observed the stack. "Do you think Donna pulled them out for some reason?"

Tali shrugged. "Either Donna did . . . or the killer."

CHAPTER
THREE

THERE WAS no way Mac was leaving right now.

Maybe he should.

Maybe it wasn't his place to be here.

But he sensed that Tali didn't mind having him. Until she told him to go, he would stay to offer emotional support.

Doc Clemson had already taken Donna's body away, but two police officers, as well as Cassidy, remained.

Tali had busied herself upstairs in her apartment by making coffee and tea for everyone. She'd also brought down some banana nut muffins. Sugar stayed faithfully at her side every moment.

Mac accepted the paper cup of coffee she handed him and took a sip.

The coffee was delicious and smooth, just as always.

Tali had a knack for making everything beautiful and tasty.

It was just one more reason to like her. Not that he needed another one.

But ever since Carol, his wife of twelve years, had died nearly three decades ago, no other woman had really caught his eye.

So Tali had caught him off guard.

He glanced out the picture window at the front of the shop. Beach Bound Books and Beans Bookstore and Coffee Shop was engraved in white on the glass, and rivulets of rain dripped down over the words, almost as if the building itself was crying and mourning.

On the boardwalk outside, Mac saw Cassidy talking to Tank Dietz.

Tank owned the surf shop next door and lived above his shop, just as Tali did.

Cassidy and Tank stood under an awning, which protected them somewhat from the rain. But the way the wind drove the downpour made it clear they wouldn't stay dry for long.

Something about their conversation made his shoulders stiffen.

Tank was talking with his hands, and he kept

glancing inside the bookstore as if to check for anyone who might be listening.

He almost looked like he felt . . . guilty.

What sense did that make?

Mac had known the guy for a long time, and he didn't seem like a killer. Besides, why would he murder a sixty-year-old bookstore owner from Hatteras Island?

His lungs tightened when Cassidy stepped back inside, and her gaze went straight to Tali.

Tali had just finished handing some coffee to another officer when she looked back. The grief in her gaze was replaced with alarm when she spotted Cassidy.

"What's going on?" Tali's voice sounded thin as she turned toward the police chief.

Cassidy remained professional, but Mac saw the telltale frown tugging at the side of her lips. "Tali, I need to ask you a few more questions."

A knot formed between Tali's eyebrows. "About what?"

"About last night."

Mac tensed.

He didn't like the sound of that.

Apprehension seized Tali at the tone of Cassidy's voice and at her question.

Why in the world would the woman want to speak with her again?

It didn't make any sense.

Unless this was just standard police procedure in these circumstances.

She had to assume that was the case.

She rolled her shoulders back. "I'd be happy to answer any questions. Whatever you need to figure out who did this to Donna."

"Would you like to talk here or down at the station?"

The question made surprise pulse through Tali in shockwaves. The station?

That seemed much more serious than talking here.

"I'm fine talking at the shop," Tali said, pulling herself together. "I don't have any secrets."

"Tank, your neighbor, said he went out with some of his friends last night. When he got back to his surf shop just after midnight, he passed your place and glanced through the window, where he saw two people arguing."

Tali blanched. "What? Like I said, I didn't hear anything. And my alarm didn't go off alerting me my door had been opened. Of course, the power went out . . ."

Cassidy tilted her head as if readying herself to dive deeper than she'd already gone. "Tali . . . Tank said he saw *you* arguing with Donna last night."

The air left Tali's lungs, and her head swirled as Cassidy's words reverberated in her mind.

Mac grabbed Tali's elbow as if knowing she needed someone to steady her before she passed out.

"What . . . ?" Tali finally asked, her gaze locking with Cassidy's. "That can't be right."

Cassidy tilted her head in an almost apologetic shrug. "Tank was certain it was you he saw. He said it was dark, but he recognized your blonde hair. Said the argument appeared heated. Is there something you're not telling me, Tali?"

Tali quickly shook her head. "I didn't come downstairs last night. I would remember it."

"Did you take any type of sleeping medication?"

"No, I try to stay away from prescriptions as much as I can. I feel like they solve one problem but cause others." She realized she was rambling and stopped. Plus, she could go on and on about that subject.

"Tali . . ."

She waited for Cassidy to continue, knowing she wouldn't like whatever else the woman had to say.

"This doesn't look good right now." Cassidy pressed her lips together, the motion only emphasizing the seriousness of this situation. "Right now, we have a witness who places you arguing with the victim right before she died in your store."

A cold chill washed through Tali at the words.

Cassidy was right.

This *didn't* look good.

What exactly was Tali supposed to do about it?

CHAPTER
FOUR

MAC DIDN'T LIKE the way this was playing out.

"Am I being arrested?" Tali's voice sounded nearly breathless.

"No. Not yet. But—"

"I'm your primary suspect." Tali pressed her eyes closed as she finished the statement.

Cassidy didn't deny the words. Mac knew they were true. So far, Tali was the one who'd had the opportunity *and* the means to murder Donna.

But there was no way Tali had motive. She didn't have it in her to take another life.

"We'll test the knife, of course. And we'll need to get your prints so they're on file."

Mac had observed the knife before Clemson took Donna's body away.

He couldn't be certain—although he was—but

that knife looked *exactly* like the ones Tali used in her kitchen.

This whole situation didn't look good.

"I'm sure my prints will be on that knife," Tali said. "I have a set that matches upstairs."

"How did it get downstairs?" Cassidy asked.

"I have no idea." She shrugged. "I'm sorry. I wish I knew. But I didn't bring it down here."

Did that mean the killer had been in her apartment? Or had Donna brought it down herself?

"And you have no idea why those books would have been left out?" Cassidy nodded toward the stack on the floor.

Tali thought about it a moment before her eyes lit with an idea. "What if those books are some type of cipher?"

Her words caught Mac off guard. "A cipher?"

Tali glanced back and forth at Mac and Cassidy, probably because they both looked at her confused.

"I know it sounds crazy," she said. "But I've read about it in books. Where there's one book that offers a code to solve some type of hidden riddle. Maybe it all ties in with that word calibrate."

"The fact that Donna handed that note to you without explanation is very curious." Cassidy let out a long breath. "Was yesterday the first time you'd ever met her?"

"It's the first time we met face-to-face. But we have an email loop with all the bookstore owners on the Outer Banks. I'd be more than happy to show you those messages. To show you my computer. Anything you need." Tali swallowed hard. "Because I didn't do this."

Just as she said the words, thunder cracked outside.

The sound made Tali jump, and she seemed to instinctively move closer to Mac, grabbing his arm as if frightened.

He didn't mind.

Sugar whined and also moved closer, brushing against his legs.

Mac was going to prove Tali was innocent if it was the last thing he did.

Three hours later, the police left.

It was still storming outside, and fingerprint dust bruised various surfaces in Tali's bookstore, which only hours before had appeared freshly cleaned and painted.

She'd been working hard to get things ready. Initially, she'd wanted to open in the spring. But a lot of people on the island had told her they'd love to have the bookstore open sooner so locals would have a place to hang out during the cold island winter.

The knotty wood floors were done, the walls painted a nautical blue, and bookshelves had been erected and stained black.

Any other day, she might feel miserable about how her pristine shop was now tainted.

But at the moment she had bigger worries.

She glanced up and saw Mac still lingering. He wore his customary olive-green utility pants and a black T-shirt that showed his muscled biceps. His gray hair was styled away from his face in a neat, no-fuss cut, and his skin bore very few wrinkles.

Usually.

Right now, lines of worry stretched across his forehead.

Tali knew he was concerned about her.

But truthfully, she was also concerned about herself.

"I don't know what I'm going to do, Mac." Her words sounded vulnerable, and she hesitantly pulled her gaze up to meet his.

Mac probably wasn't the person she needed to share that with. Yet, she also felt like he was the best person she could have on her side to help her figure this out.

Police Chief Chambers seemed fair, like a good

and capable person who'd remain objective and do her job to the best of her ability.

But Tali sensed that Mac had her back, even if that thought was crazy considering their past circumstances.

Mac lowered his voice and said, "We're going to figure out who really killed Donna."

Momentary hope filled her. "We are? How?"

"We need to ask questions. Figure out who on Lantern Beach knew Donna was on the island. Figure out who might have motive."

Her heart raced with possibility.

If there was one thing she hated it was sitting back and doing nothing—especially when there was a lot to be done.

She *loved* his plan.

"Okay." Her voice lilted. "Where do we start?"

"First, we start by cleaning up down here." He glanced at the area where Donna had been found. "The police released the scene."

Tali frowned. That was the last thing she wanted to do.

But Mac was right. This needed to be cleaned up —especially the puddle of blood in the middle of her newly refinished wood floor.

"I'll tell you what," Mac continued. "If you get

me some cleaning supplies, I'll get started down here."

"And I can help . . ."

He took her shoulders and turned her toward the stairs. "While I do this, I want you to rest."

"I'm not good at resting. Besides, I can't ask you to clean all this up."

"You didn't ask. I'm offering. How about if you make me some chocolate chip cookies instead? Then we'll call it even."

Her heart fluttered. "You'd do that for me?"

"Of course."

"Thank you." Her voice cracked under the weight of her gratitude.

"After this, I say we talk to the two other book-store owners that stayed on the island last night."

"Gia and Alice."

"Yes, Gia and Alice. You said that Donna didn't have any other friends here, right? That's why she stayed with you."

Tali nodded. "That's what she said."

"Then maybe we can call Gia and Alice and see if we can talk to them. I'm sure Cassidy will want to talk to them also. You gave her their names and phone numbers, right?"

"I did when I gave my statement." She paused. "Should I call them?"

"Yes, certainly. Tell them that as soon as the police chief talks to them, you need them to come here. It sounds like we all need to have a buzz fest. Some discourse. A groupthink."

Tali stared at him with narrowed eyes.

Mac shrugged. "I've been hanging out with Axel some in my free time. He's teaching me all the newest slang. It's *fire*. Or, as Axel says, *Fiya*."

Tali smiled. Axel Hendrix worked for an organization here on the island called Blackout. A former Navy SEAL who loved motorcycles, he was a reformed ladies' man who was now happily dating Olivia Rollins.

Tali released her breath.

Maybe they could track down some answers.

But it seemed like whatever they found out . . . none of that would explain why Tank said he had seen Tali arguing with Donna downstairs last night, something she simply hadn't done.

CHAPTER
FIVE

MAC HAD FINISHED CLEANING, Tali had made some cookies, and Gia and Alice were on their way over—riding together.

As Mac sat on the couch with Sugar, he realized that he *really* wanted to talk to Tank. But he didn't want to leave Tali right now. So that conversation would have to wait.

It was a shame that the security cameras had gone out. Had the killer known that? Had he or she known about the video monitoring outside Tali's shop and seen the opportunity to strike during the power outage?

Or had it all been planned out and premeditated?

Or what if Donna wasn't the actual target? What if she'd just been a victim of circumstance? If someone had come into the bookstore looking for something when Donna had stumbled upon him or her?

There were so many questions, and they hadn't even begun to skim the surface of this investigation yet.

When Tali went to freshen up, Mac made her a turkey and cheese sandwich. He felt awkward poking around in her kitchen, but it seemed the least he could do. Tali was always busy taking care of everyone else. But sometimes even the caretaker needed to be taken care of.

Twenty minutes later, she emerged from her room, the scent of flowery perfume floating out with her. He set the sandwich on the table and fixed her a glass of ice water.

Her eyes lit when she saw the sandwich. "For me?"

"I thought you could use something in your stomach."

"I'm not sure if I can eat, but I'll try." She sat down and glanced up at him. "Thank you."

"Of course."

"Aren't you going to eat also?"

"I'm not that hungry." Mac sat at the table across from her, watching her for any signs of shock.

He knew this was a lot to handle. First, the dead

body, and then being accused of the crime. It could take a toll on a person.

She closed her eyes to lift a silent prayer before taking a bite of her turkey and cheese.

Then she glanced up at him again. "Thank you for all of this. I really do appreciate it."

Mac wanted to tell her that she was worth it. That he'd love to do things like this for her every day.

But this wasn't the time to mention it. Maybe there never would be a time.

However, he needed to say *something*.

He opened his mouth. But before any words escaped, a knock sounded at the shop's door.

He glanced at the time.

If his guess was correct, Alice and Gia had arrived.

Maybe they could help provide some answers.

———

Tali wasn't sure if she was relieved to see Alice and Gia or not.

Cassidy had already talked to them, so they knew about Donna. When they'd arrived, both had stared into her shop as if trying to picture Donna there.

They were trying to imagine the scene while Tali kept trying to forget.

Tali had quickly ushered them upstairs and into her living room, where they sat on the two couches there.

Their expressions were a mix of mourning, curiosity, and maybe even a little anger.

Mac had been a doll and fixed them all drinks. He'd even set out some of the chocolate chip cookies Tali had made earlier.

"I just can't believe this." Gia shook her head, her oversized hoop earrings clanging against her jaw.

"I can't either." Alice rubbed her arms as if chilled. "Who would do something like this?"

"That's what I'm trying to figure out." Tali drew her legs beneath her and sighed. "I'm not going to beat around the bush. I'm sure you both know that it doesn't look good for me. Donna died in *my* bookstore . . . *while* staying with me . . . and the police assume *I* was the last person to talk to her."

Gia and Alice both shifted as if Tali's words made them uncomfortable.

Certainly, they didn't think she was guilty, did they?

In all honesty, these two really didn't know her that well. Sure, they had a bond since they all loved books and owned bookstores here on the islands.

But not enough time had passed for them to build a significant level of trust.

"You both knew Donna better than Tali did." Mac stepped into the conversation as if he sensed Tali faltering. "Did she have any enemies?"

"None that I know of." Alice shrugged. "She lived a fairly quiet life. Had never been married. No children. No hobbies other than books."

"I agree," Gia said. "She had one of those strange personalities that made her neither likable nor unlikable. She was just . . . almost unnoticeable—except when her paranoia kicked in."

"Paranoia?" Mac asked.

Alice let out a long breath. "She was just always jumpy, always expecting the worst, I suppose."

"What are we going to do?" Gia rubbed her arms. "All I really want is to go home to Ocracoke. But I can't. Not with the weather like it is. I knew I should've never come here."

Her words caused Tali to pause. "You didn't want to come?"

Apology instantly filled Gia's gaze. "That's not what I meant. It's just that . . ." She waved her hand in the air as if brushing off the question. "It's really nothing."

Maybe her words were true. But Tali had a feeling Gia had been about to say more before she realized how her words might sound.

Did Gia know something that might help pinpoint the real killer?

If so, Tali needed to find out exactly what that was.

Her future might depend on it.

CHAPTER
SIX

"WELL, I don't know about you guys, but I'm exhausted," Tali muttered.

Gia patted her legs before rising from her chair and stretching. "Me too."

Alice followed suit and stood also.

Mac remained in the kitchen, where he'd slipped to earlier to give the women their space. But he was still keeping an eye on everything and making mental notes as he wiped down the counters and straightened up a bit.

He tried not to be too obvious. Instead, he needed to appear as if he were simply a supportive friend—which he was. He was a supportive friend with more than thirty years of police experience.

"If you need anything, you let us know." Gia

clutched Tali's hand, her brown eyes glimmering with overblown grief.

"Absolutely," Alice echoed. "We're here for you, Tali. When one in our circle suffers, we all do."

Tali thanked them before walking them downstairs.

Mac moved to the window and watched as they ran through the rain to their vehicle.

When Tali returned upstairs, she paused in front of Mac.

He fully expected her to say she needed to lie down—a polite way of asking him to leave.

But her expression changed. "I want to talk to Tank."

Mac raised an eyebrow, surprised at her burst of energy. "I thought you said you were exhausted."

"I am, and I'm glad they didn't stay any longer. But only because I don't have time to sit around all day. I need to figure out what happened before I end up in jail."

Mac resisted a smile. He liked the way Tali thought.

In fact, he liked everything about her.

He shifted before asking his next question. "Do you mind if I go with you?"

"I was hoping you'd ask."

They shared a grin before going downstairs, grabbing an umbrella from behind the door and stepping outside.

An unrelenting wind whipped around them.

They huddled together under the umbrella, Mac giving more coverage to Tali than he kept for himself. It was the gentlemanly thing to do.

Since it was October, there weren't many tourists here on the island now. Some stores were still open, hoping for last-minute sales before the holidays. January, February, and March seemed to be dead retail-wise.

Mac and Tali dashed together to Tank's store next door. The lights were on, indicating the Riptide Surf Shop was open.

As they stepped inside, Mac closed the umbrella then set it in the corner so water wouldn't drip everywhere.

Tali pushed her hair back from her face, taking a quick moment to compose herself.

Mac's gaze stopped on Tank, who stood behind the counter. A strange expression crossed the surfer's face.

It almost looked as if Tank were nervous. As if he really thought Tali might be a killer.

This guy truly believed what he thought he saw last night was accurate, didn't he?

That was evident by watching him now.

Mac made a mental note of that.

His gaze traveled to the woman working here, Tank's new employee, Peggy. Despite her old-fashioned name, the woman was in her twenties. Her blonde hair was knotted into dreadlocks, and she liked to hit the waves whenever she could.

Her nose ring, lack of makeup, and tanned skin made Mac peg her for one of the island's many beach bums.

Other than that, he didn't know much about her.

"Tali . . . Mac . . ." Tank paused from sorting through some clothes hangers, his voice even raspier than usual. "I wasn't expecting to see the two of you here."

Mac stepped closer, sensing Tali's nerves and knowing he should take the lead. "This weather is a real beast, isn't it?"

"You can say that again." Tank stepped from around the counter and shoved his hands into the pockets of his jeans.

The man looked like anything but a tank. In fact, he got his nickname because he loved wearing tank tops—even in the winter. He had a shaved head, a scraggly goatee, and what appeared to be permanent sunglass lines around his eyes.

His gaze fluttered back and forth between the two of them. "You guys doing okay? I heard you had more excitement over at your place last night, Mrs. Robinson."

That was right. *More excitement.*

During the renovation process, skeletal remains had been found behind one of Tali's walls. Then just last month, someone had given Tali an incomplete manuscript which detailed crimes that had begun to play out on the island.

"We're fine." Tali stood more stiffly than usual, which was to be expected considering the circumstances. "And, please, call me Tali."

"That's crazy about that woman." Peggy's voice sounded cool and aloof, and the scent of patchouli floated around her. "A knife in her back? Isn't that the definition of being stabbed in the back?"

Mac didn't know how to respond, so he didn't. Instead, he moved on.

He turned back to Tank. "I was hoping we could ask you some questions."

Tank's gaze drifted to Tali again. "Sure."

But he sounded uncertain.

"I already know what you told the police." Tali had a motherly tone to her voice.

Even though she had no kids or grandkids, she naturally had a nurturing personality. When she wasn't in situations like this, she had a wide smile and fluid actions and a way of talking with her hands in an animated way that captured people's attention. Mac could easily imagine her doing story time for children once her shop opened.

Tank's voice sank low as an apologetic expression captured his face. "I'm sorry, Mrs. . . . Tali. But I couldn't lie to the police about what I saw."

"I don't want you to lie." Tali softened her voice. "But I didn't kill that woman, Tank."

Tank shrugged and took a step back. Was the action out of fear? Resignation?

Mac wasn't sure.

"I don't know what to say," Tank finally said. "She looked just like you."

"It was dark," Tali said. "The power was out. Could you even see that well into the shop?"

He shrugged again. "I don't know. I mean, yes, it was dark, and it was raining. But lightning flashed several times, and I caught glimpses of what was going on inside. The blonde hair is kind of unmistakable."

Mac frowned at his words. They were true. The whole thing *did* seem very suspicious. But he knew Tali was innocent.

"Could you hear anything over the storm?" Mac asked.

Tank let out a long breath and then glanced outside. "It was hard to make out anything. Once I saw it was an argument, I didn't want to draw any attention to myself. But I thought I heard one of the women say, 'You should've never come here.'"

———————

Tali couldn't stop thinking about what Tank had said. About how it looked as if Tali had been arguing with Donna.

You should've never come here.

Cassidy hadn't mentioned that. Then again, Cassidy probably couldn't tell them everything when it came to an investigation. But still, the words were interesting.

They showed a connection between Donna and the killer.

Mac escorted Tali back to her place.

He put the umbrella away before turning to her. Then he opened his mouth as if he were about to say something. Before any words left his lips, his phone beeped.

His lips twitched with a frown as he pulled the device from his pocket and glanced at the screen. "It's one of the town council members. We need to have an emergency meeting about the power outage. I sent them all a message earlier this morning before I left and . . ." He shrugged as if he felt guilty. "This can't wait."

"I understand. You've already done a lot. Thank you." She meant the words.

She watched him leave before locking the door and stepping back.

As she glanced around the once-cozy shop, she shivered.

This place was supposed to be a fresh start. A new beginning. A chance to reinvent herself.

But now it was becoming a place of nightmares.

Just as she'd done when she first arrived on Lantern Beach, Tali questioned her decision about coming. About selling everything she had back in South Carolina and investing it all into this shop.

What if that decision was a mistake?

She didn't have a backup plan. She'd only known she needed a change from being a librarian and living in the same town where she'd been for so long.

A bookstore/coffee shop on Lantern Beach seemed like the perfect opportunity.

But what if that decision cost her more than she'd bargained for?

CHAPTER
SEVEN

JUST AS TALI put some baked potato soup on for dinner, a knock sounded at her door. Sugar began barking at her, urging her to answer.

Back when she'd lived in South Carolina, she remembered feeling excited whenever someone stopped by to visit.

Since moving to Lantern Beach, unexpected visits usually meant something was wrong.

She walked across her apartment and peered out the window onto the boardwalk.

The tension left her shoulders when she saw the three gals standing at her door.

Her book club.

They must have heard what happened, and now they were here to offer their support.

Warmth filled her at the thought. These three girls

—even though they were all considerably younger than Tali—had brought her so much joy since coming here.

The women were as different as a gardening book was to a suspense novel.

Serena was a part-time reporter and part-time ice cream lady who loved mysteries—real life ones preferably. Her dog, Scoops, and Sugar had become best buddies lately. The girl was quirky and some-times pushy, but she had a good heart.

Abby Mendez had only moved to the island this summer. She was a community theater actress who was trying to start a theater troupe on the island. She often practiced different accents during everyday conversation, and her extroverted side picked up the slack during any lags in conversation.

And finally, there was Cadence Garth. Her cousin, Lisa Dillinger, owned The Crazy Chefette restaurant. Cadence, the quietest of the group, had moved here to help Lisa with her two children as well as fill in at the restaurant.

Tali rushed down the steps, Sugar on her heels, and threw open the door.

The three gals all rushed inside carrying the customary treats they seemed to bring whenever they came, even though Tali always insisted they didn't have to.

Hugs went around as well as murmurs of condolences.

Then Tali ushered them upstairs.

Usually, they stayed down in the coffee shop area to talk.

But not this time.

Once they were settled upstairs, the real conversation began—as they all shared some soup, of course.

The girls asked a lot of questions about what had happened, and Tali filled them in on all the details.

No one had told her she couldn't.

It almost felt as if she were telling the story around a campfire the way they all listened and nodded. Their mouths formed circles of horror, and gasps left their lips. At times, their hands covered their hearts and they leaned back with shock.

"I have a question." Cadence set her spoon in the soup bowl and pushed it away from her. "You said there was a stack of books beside her body? Which ones?"

Tali eased back in her seat. When she glanced at the books after finding Donna, she'd tried to commit the titles to memory.

But unfortunately, her memory wasn't as good as it used to be. That was evident by the fact she'd worn two different sandals out when she'd run to the store the other day.

She *could* blame that on age, but she'd always been a bit flighty with those things—especially when preoccupied. Getting her shop ready had definitely engrossed her thoughts lately.

She gave Sugar a good head rub as she tried to remember. "Let's see. There was *Betrayed* by Lisa Scottoline, *Danger Is Everywhere* by David O'Doherty, *Misery* by Stephen King, *Shadow of the Storm* by Connilyn Cosette, and *Lies We Tell Ourselves* by Amy Matayo."

"What could the connection possibly be between all of those books?" Serena tapped her finger against her lips. "They're not even the same genre. You have a thriller along with a women's fiction title, a historical novel, a psychological horror, and a children's book. It doesn't make any sense."

Tali shared her theory that maybe one of the books was being used as a cipher.

"I think it's a good theory, but wouldn't you need more than words to do that?" Cadence asked. "I actually think they also use numbers. Page numbers combined with line numbers, maybe? Combined with the number corresponding to the word's position on the line?"

Tali frowned. "I think you're right. I wasn't thinking that one through, I guess."

"I'd be happy to see if I can find copies of those

books," Abby said. "Maybe we can pour through them and see if there *is* some type of connection."

"I'm sure Cassidy is also doing that since I mentioned the theory to her and she took the books to the station. But feel free."

"Wait a second . . ." Serena sat up straighter. "Can I have a piece of paper?"

Tali found some in the drawer of the end table along with a pen and handed them to her. Then she sat back down at the table, anxious to see where Serena was going with this.

Serena quickly scribbled down the book titles and then stared at the list.

"Do you remember what order they were in?" she asked after a moment.

Tali tilted her head as she thought it through. Finally, she blurted them off in the order she thought they were in. "*Shadow of the Storm, Betrayed, Lies We Tell Ourselves, Misery, Danger Is Everywhere.*"

She thought she had the order correct.

Maybe her memory was better than she thought.

Serena scribbled furiously.

"What are you getting at?" Tali studied Serena a moment, hoping she wasn't simply being dramatic.

Sometimes Serena was known for her shenanigans. The girl had no fear and wasn't easily embarrassed. Plus, once she got an idea, it was hard to change her mind.

"This is book spine poetry," she announced, a victorious look fluttering through her gaze. "The killer left a message using the spines of these books."

A chill washed through Tali.

Serena was right!

Book spine poetry was a rage among book lovers.

But the message left was *not* comforting.

Betrayed? Danger? Storm? Misery? Lies?

Whoever had left those books was definitely trying to send a message.

Mac checked his messages and saw Tali had left him one, asking him to call her as soon as his meeting was over.

He was happy to hear from her but, unfortunately, knowing the two of them needed to talk made his meeting feel like it was taking even longer.

Still, as mayor it was his job to run this town, and he couldn't shirk his responsibility.

But it was past dinnertime by the time they wrapped up.

As soon as Mac got back to his office and closed the door, he gave Tali a call. He watched the rain running down the window as he waited for her to answer.

Thankfully, she did so on the first ring.

"Tali, it's Mac. What's going on?"

She told him about the book spine poetry message that had been left.

He squinted at her description. "Book spine poetry? I've never heard of such a thing."

That was beside the point right now.

He had to admit, he was impressed the ladies had figured that out. He gave them mental kudos.

"Did you tell Cassidy about this?" He leaned his hip against his desk, his blood now pumping with anticipation.

"She was the first person I called," Tali confirmed. "It only seemed wise."

"I agree. It's an interesting twist, that's for sure. One I've never seen before in all my years of police work." He paused as he chewed on that thought.

"What is it?" Tali's voice caught as she waited.

"There's one thing that's bugging me." He rubbed his chin as he tried to put the pieces together. "How does book spine poetry tie in with the word *calibrate*?"

Tali sighed. "I'm not sure. That doesn't make sense to me either. But . . . in order to calibrate something to make it accurate you have to compare it to something else that's standard, right?"

He straightened and began pacing his office. "Yes, that's true."

"Could it be the books are only part of the cipher? Maybe there's something we need to compare it to in order to find the answers."

"That's what we need to figure out."

Mac would probably be tossing ideas around all night tonight instead of sleeping. If ADHD had been a thing when Mac was a kid, he would have *definitely* been diagnosed.

"Keep thinking about it," he told Tali. "Maybe something will come to you. In the meantime, I hope you're able to get some rest tonight."

"Me too." Tali's voice wavered as if everything was beginning to get to her.

He paused as another idea hit him. "Would you like me to come check things out at your place before I head home?"

She was quiet a moment as if considering his words. Finally, she said, "No, I'll be fine. I've locked my doors, and the power is back on now so my cameras should work. But thank you. I appreciate your thoughtfulness."

Mac would be lying if he said he wasn't disappointed. However, he'd respect her wishes.

"Of course," Mac told her. "But if you need anything, call me."

"I will. And thank you."

He only hoped that trouble stayed far, far away from her.

CHAPTER
EIGHT

TALI HADN'T SLEPT WELL last night. She'd tried. But every time she thought she heard a sound, she jumped. The storm still raged outside, the winds coming and going in waves.

As of last night, the ferry was still closed. The weather system was causing huge swells in the ocean, which meant it wasn't safe to be out on the water. Forecasters were saying it might be like this for a couple more days.

That meant Gia and Alice would still be stuck here.

One thought nagged Tali as she sat down on her couch by the picture window with her morning coffee.

One bookstore owner hadn't been able to make it to their meeting. Jeannine Hailey. She owned The

Story Keeper up in Nags Head. It would have meant traveling nearly all day for her to come.

Tali couldn't help but wonder if she might know something. She'd heard Jeannine, Gia, Donna, and Alice got together weekly in the off season.

"What do you think, Sugar? Should I call Jeannine?" She glanced at her dog as he sat beside her on the sofa.

He panted before barking his affirmation.

Tali rubbed his head. "Good answer."

At nine o'clock—a reasonable hour to call somebody—Tali dialed the woman's number.

Jeannine answered on the first ring.

She'd already heard about Donna.

"I've got to say, I really wanted to make the meeting." Jeannine sounded brisk and all business.

She'd been the CEO of a successful financial company before giving that up for a simpler life on the beach. But touches of her business sense often emerged during conversations.

"But now I'm kind of glad that I didn't," Jeannine finished. "What happened is so terrible."

"I know. I didn't know Donna that well. Not at all, really. This was the first time we'd met in person. But I can't believe she's dead. And I can't believe how she died."

"God rest her soul."

Tali set her coffee on the end table and pulled her legs beneath her. "Listen, can you tell me something?"

"Whatever you need."

"Do you know if Donna had any enemies?"

"You mean, besides Gia?"

Tali sucked in a breath. "Wait a minute . . . Gia and Donna didn't get along?"

"I thought you knew. It's not like it's a secret, at least."

"Why didn't they get along?"

Jeannine let out a sigh. "It seemed really trivial, actually. But Gia had planned this big advertising campaign for her store involving a scavenger hunt. It was supposed to start two weeks after the advertisements went out. Well, only a week later, Donna had a scavenger hunt in her store—there were a lot of similarities. Donna claimed she got the idea online. Gia insisted Donna stole it from her. They feuded about it for quite a while. Gia was *not* happy, but Donna didn't back down either."

A new suspect took root in her mind.

Where exactly was Gia when Donna was murdered? Who had she said she'd been staying with? Someone named Wanda?

Tali intended on finding out.

But there was only one problem.

Gia didn't look anything like Tali, and Tank had said he saw a blonde with Donna.

Mac had more meetings that morning.

But his mind was on what had happened yesterday.

It was a pleasant surprise when, before lunchtime, his phone rang, and he saw it was Tali.

He tried to sound casual as he answered. "Hey, Tali."

"Good morning, Mac. I hope I'm not bothering you."

"Never. But I have a feeling you're not calling just to pass time. You have something on your mind."

"I do. What are you doing on your lunch break?"

Against his wishes, his pulse spiked at the fleeting possibility that she might ask him to eat with her. "Nothing. Why are you asking?"

"Any chance you want to do an errand with me?"

He didn't want to say yes too quickly and sound desperate, so he paused. Axel—while the two of them had breakfast at The Crazy Chefette last week —had taken it upon himself to teach Mac the basics of modern dating.

Make sure your dating app picture looks like you in real life.

That one was easy because Mac had no desire to meet someone online.

Careful what you post on your socials. It will always come back to you. Always.

That one also wasn't a problem since Mac stayed off social media.

Don't always communicate by text. Women like to hear your voice.

At least, Mac could agree with that one.

Maybe Mac paused for too long because, a moment later, Tali said, "It involves cake."

"Then by all means, yes. I'm definitely in." He let out a chuckle, hoping she could hear his playfulness.

"Great." Warmth saturated her voice. "Can you meet me at my place in two hours?"

"I'd be more than happy to. But do you want to tell me what's really going on?"

"I will. When you get here."

Now Mac was more curious than ever.

CHAPTER
NINE

TALI'S THOUGHTS continued to turn over in her mind as she waited for Mac to show up and as she put the finishing touches on her lemon pound cakes.

They'd always been one of Jimmy's favorites, so it seemed weird now that she was making an extra one for Mac.

Tali frowned, trying not to overthink it.

One thing was certain: she had to stop baking.

When she'd reached her forties, she'd realized that eating as if she were in her twenties would no longer work. That's when she'd decided that even bookworms needed to exercise.

She'd started Publishing Pilates at her library, where patrons joined her three times a week for an hour, and they listened to speakers talk about publishing while working out. A walking club had formed where book lovers walked together at parks while listening to a chosen audiobook and then gathered afterward to discuss it. Then she'd formed the Books Boot Camp and Barre Studio Books.

The possibilities had seemed endless.

They'd all been a hit, and they'd all encouraged Tali to stay in shape while engaging in her favorite activity—books and reading.

She'd been thinking all morning, ever since she talked to Jeannine, about how she could find out more information on Gia.

Finally, Tali had decided to go pay her a visit. When Gia and Alice had stopped by earlier, Tali had casually asked them where they were staying. Now, she was glad she had.

But she needed a good reason to visit, and cake *always* seemed like a good excuse to visit.

Other questions still swirled in her head.

Did Donna stack those books into the book spine poetry before she died? They were all books that Tali had ordered and set out on her shelves for when the store opened.

Or had the killer been behind it?

And what did "calibrate" mean?

Why would Donna have given her that word and told her not to open the envelope until the next morning? Had she suspected something might happen?

But she hadn't acted like she was in any danger.

Nothing made sense.

Which led Tali to another thought.

What if she—meaning Tali herself—was being framed?

It seemed like a crazy idea because she hadn't been on the island long enough to make anyone angry. Unless you included the two other crimes that had happened in relation to her, but those culprits were already behind bars.

But the killer had used Tali's kitchen knife and left it there as evidence. And how else could she explain the fact that this killer supposedly looked like her?

Unless it truly had been raining so hard outside that Tank hadn't seen inside of the shop clearly.

Then there was the note Donna had left her. Donna certainly hadn't been trying to frame Tali for her murder . . . right? That didn't make any sense.

Still feeling unsettled, Tali wrapped the final lemon pound cake in some plastic wrap and placed it in a paper gift bag with Beach Bound Books and Beans across the front.

She went downstairs just as Mac arrived.

Now it was time to pretend she was Nancy Drew.

And there was no shame in that.

But if things turned south, she might have to resort to pretending she was Stephanie Plum instead.

———————

Mac was thankful for a pocket of sunshine during the otherwise stormy weekend.

Gray clouds still churned in the distance. But, for now, the sun's rays filled the sky.

And there was Tali.

She looked beautiful as she grinned at him from the doorway of her bookshop. She held out a bright, cheerful yellow bag and handed it to him. "This cake is for you."

"Cake?" He offered a slight bow. "Thank you. And you have more?"

Tali offered a wide grin and held up another bag. "This involves the next part of my plan."

Mac was more curious than ever. "Okay then. You have my attention now. Where are we heading?"

With Tali's free hand, she took a piece of paper from her pocket and rattled off an address.

"That's not too far away." He glanced at the sky. "If you want to, we can risk walking. But with the weather around here you never know. It could be raining by the time we start back."

"I think walking sounds like a great idea. On the beach, of course, right?"

"It's a better workout that way." He held up his bag. "You mind if I leave mine here?"

"Not at all."

After he set his bag inside, Tali and Mac began their walk. They veered off the boardwalk and onto the sandy shore. Thankfully, today the sand was packed more than it sometimes was. The grains on the island's shores fluctuated between being loose and sugar-like and packed more like dirt.

Several people were on the beach, a few Mac recognized.

Including the woman walking toward them now.

Aubrey Jones.

Mac slowed as the woman got closer.

Aubrey was thin with petite features and a rather youthful appearance. Her dark-brown hair was cut to her chin with bangs feathering across her forehead.

She was a staple here in the community, and Mac had known her for years—back even before her husband died nearly a decade ago.

"Fancy seeing you two here." Aubrey glanced at Mac and then nodded at Tali. "Thanks for having me and the other ladies over for tea a while back. It was really nice."

Aubrey was one of the widows who attended

church with Tali. There was actually quite a large community of single senior adults on the island.

Mac didn't usually hang out with them. Not because he didn't like them, but usually because he was caught up in other matters. Matters concerning the town or helping Cassidy or keeping his physical prowess up to date.

"I heard what happened." Aubrey frowned and pushed her hair from her eyes. The wind immediately blew it back. "Another dead body."

Tali frowned. "I can't believe it either."

"Did I hear that it was Donna Winters from Hatteras?"

Mac tilted his head. "Did you know Donna?"

She shrugged. "Not personally. But her ex-boyfriend lives here. I went out with him a few times a couple of years ago."

Now Aubrey had Mac's full attention. "Is that right?"

"I mean, if Police Chief Chambers looked it up, it wouldn't be on record, of course. But they dated for a good couple of years. Donna would come here to Lantern Beach to visit him, and he'd go to Hatteras to visit her."

"What exactly is the name of this ex-boyfriend?" Mac asked.

"Ed Hauser."

Ed Hauser? Mac knew the guy. The man was in his late fifties, and he owned a roofing company on the island. As far as Mac knew, he'd never been in trouble with the law. In fact, the man mostly just minded his own business.

"Good to know," Mac finally muttered.

Aubrey turned her gaze back to Tali. "I can't wait for your shop to open. It's going to be a wonderful addition to Lantern Beach."

"Thank you." Tali offered a smile. "I appreciate that."

But something about the look on Aubrey's face didn't quite come across as sincere.

CHAPTER
TEN

TALI FELT an emotion she'd long since retired rearing its ugly head again.

Was that jealousy?

She guffawed at the thought. No. She was not the jealous type. And she most certainly was *not* jealous of Aubrey Jones.

Tali must just be unsettled by all that had been going on.

That had to be it.

Sure, the woman was beautiful. And charming. And she had a successful HVAC business that her late husband had started on the island.

But none of those things bothered Tali.

No, it was the way she looked at Mac that had Tali rattled.

And *that* was something ridiculous to feel jealous about.

Tali and Mac were just friends—if that. Besides, there was no chance of a future between them, even if she did feel their bond growing.

She reminded herself to keep Mac at a distance.

But not right now.

Right now, they were going to go talk to Gia.

"Aubrey seems nice," Tali said as they started down the beach again.

"She is," Mac said. "A real staple here in town. I could see the two of you getting along well."

"Oh, yeah? Well, I may have had a run of bad luck crime-wise here on the island, but I certainly can't complain about the friendships I've made since I arrived."

She had a feeling Aubrey wouldn't be one of them.

Tali couldn't help but wonder if the two had ever dated.

Aubrey was *definitely* interested.

But was Mac?

Why did that thought make Tali feel a twinge of jealousy again? It was ridiculous.

But Tali could see where Mac could be interested.

Before she could dwell on the thought Mac

pointed to a yellow, modest-sized house in the distance. "Here it is."

They climbed up the steps to the front door, and Tali rang the bell.

A moment later, a woman answered—a woman who was not Gia. But the two of them could be sisters. They shared the same olive skin, dark hair, and wide smile.

"I'm sorry to intrude," Tali started. "We were hoping we might be able to talk to Gia."

"Oh." Realization washed over her face. "You're the new bookstore owner, aren't you?"

Tali raised her hand. "That's me." Her voice lilted upward. "I'm Tali. And this is Mac."

"Yes, I recognize the mayor. So nice to meet you both. I'm Wanda." She twisted her neck before calling, "Gia! Come here. You have visitors."

The woman's volume *definitely* matched Gia's. Both were loud.

Wanda ushered them inside, explaining, "Just in case it starts raining again."

A moment later, Gia appeared. Surprise washed over the woman's features as soon as she spotted Tali and Mac.

Gia's gaze bounced back and forth between Tali and Mac, almost as if nervous. "What brings you here?"

Tali handed her the gift bag. "I know that this has all been a lot on you since you and Donna went way back. So I thought I'd bring something to cheer you up. I made one for Alice as well."

Gia peered inside and saw the lemon pound cake. "This is very thoughtful of you. Thank you. It smells delicious." She paused. "Any update on what happened to Donna?"

Tali shook her head. "Not that I've heard. How about you?"

Gia shook her head also. "Nothing here."

Tali rubbed her arms—honestly chilled at the memory of finding Donna. She'd never forget the sight of the woman's dead body. "I still can't believe any of this happened."

"None of us can," Wanda said. "And you didn't hear any of it? You were just upstairs, right?"

"I know that it seems weird, but I didn't hear anything," Tali said. "Did you two sleep through the storm?"

"We turned in around ten p.m.," Wanda said, clearly a talker. "But I know when I saw Gia the next morning, she didn't look like she'd gotten a wink of sleep." She glanced at Gia. "Did you have nightmares that night?"

Gia's cheeks lost some of their color. "I never sleep well during storms."

Wanda slapped her friend's arm in a jovial manner. "Girl . . . is that right? Why didn't I ever know that about you?"

Gia let out a weak laugh. "I don't know. Guess the subject never came up."

Or did Wanda really not know because Gia had just made that up? Tali stored that possibility in the back of her mind.

Now Tali needed to figure out how to bring up the subject of Gia's fight with Donna.

She shifted as she glanced at Gia. "You know Jeannine Hailey?"

"Of course." Gia stiffened. "Why?"

"I actually talked to her earlier. She told me about the tension between you and Donna. I would have never guessed. Anyway, I'm so sorry to hear things ended on such a sour note between the two of you."

Gia's eyes widened. "Jeannine told you that?"

"She made it sound like your disagreement was public knowledge."

"She had no right to say anything." Gia crossed her arms and scowled. "It wasn't any of her business."

"I'm sorry. I didn't realize you would take offense." Although Tali *did* have a good idea that she might have this reaction.

"I do wish we'd had time to make amends. But it

is what it is. I'm sorry Donna is no longer with us. Now, if you don't mind, I'm feeling tired and need to go lie down."

Tali nodded.

Gia was definitely hiding something.

The question was . . . what?

"She's hiding something," Mac said as they stepped away from the house.

He directed Tali toward the beach. But as soon as they crossed the dune line, the wind picked up.

"I agree," Tali said. "What isn't Gia telling us?"

He glanced at the sky again. The storm would be on them soon unless they picked up their pace.

He took Tali's arm and led her a little faster. "Whatever it is, we're going to have to find out ourselves. She won't be sharing."

Tali glanced at him, something dancing through her gaze.

Was it because Mac had said *we*? Because Mac had made a verbal admission that he was helping her?

There was a good chance that was true.

"I guess it's good news that Cassidy hasn't stopped by today to ask me more questions. Does that mean I'm not her number one suspect anymore?" Hope climbed through Tali's voice.

Mac bit back a frown.

He wanted to reassure Tali and tell her that was true. But he couldn't.

He'd checked in with Cassidy earlier, and he knew the police chief didn't have any other suspects besides Tali. He didn't want to give Tali false hope that she should relax.

"I know Cassidy is still working on collecting evidence."

Raindrops began pelting them.

"Come on!" Mac took her hand and began pulling her across the sand.

She let out a squeal—possibly of delight—as she ran behind him.

Finally, they reached the bookstore. Tali unlocked the door, and they rushed inside.

Mac nearly felt exhilarated—and based on the look on Tali's face, so did she.

She let out a laugh as she pushed her wet hair from her face and glanced up at him. She looked youthful and almost carefree.

It was only then he realized how close they were standing.

Close enough to run his fingers along her jaw.

To see the flecks in her eyes.

To kiss her.

Time felt suspended for a moment as he pondered what to do. One wrong move could cause major ripple effects.

None of which would be good.

CHAPTER
ELEVEN

JUST WHEN TALI thought things couldn't feel any more awkward, someone knocked at the door.

Police Chief Chambers.

Alarm rushed through her.

Something about the woman's expression made Tali feel ill, almost as if Cassidy were here bearing bad news.

Tali pulled her sweater closer around her as she opened the door and ushered Cassidy inside. "What a surprise."

She sounded polite, even though panic tried to claim her. And her wet clothes only deepened the chill sweeping through her.

"Mac. Tali." She nodded at both of them.

"We found out something," Tali rushed. She then told Cassidy about Ed Hauser.

Cassidy promised to look into him and then said, "I have an update for you also. Would you like to speak somewhere private?"

Tali's gaze shot to Mac as she considered her options. She wanted him by her side.

Was that crazy?

Maybe.

But it was the truth.

"I'm fine right here." Tali nodded with decision.

"Very well." Cassidy offered another quick nod. "Tali, I wanted to let you know that we got the fingerprints back from the knife that was found in Donna's back."

"And?" Tali held her breath as she waited for Cassidy's response.

A frown tugged at the side of the police chief's lips. "Your fingerprints were all over it."

"Tali admitted to using it earlier." Mac's chest expanded protectively. "It's a knife from her kitchen."

"I know." Cassidy shrugged. "Donna's prints were also found on it."

"Maybe she heard something and grabbed it before she went downstairs to check it out . . ." Tali suggested. "But I would think she would've woken me up first."

She supposed they would never know what

Donna was thinking at the time, especially since she was no longer here to speak for herself.

Cassidy lowered her voice. "I know you, Tali, and I don't think you would do something like this. It's just that all the evidence . . ."

"Is stacking up," Tali finished.

Cassidy nodded somberly. "Yes, it's stacking up. Your store. Your friend. Your knife. And you were the last one seen with Donna."

"But I wasn't the one downstairs arguing with her." Panic pulsed through Tali's blood. "I don't even have a motive. You've got to know that."

Cassidy didn't say anything.

Tali's thoughts continued to race.

"I'm going to need you to stay in town until further notice," Cassidy said.

Did that mean an arrest warrant was coming soon?

Memories of when Jimmy was arrested flooded back to Tali. She wanted to believe the justice system was fair and that only the guilty were punished. But she'd seen firsthand how that wasn't true.

That's why Tali could find no comfort in this situation.

Her thoughts still raced as Cassidy left.

But Mac lingered a moment longer.

As Sugar barked from upstairs, more alarming thoughts hit Tali.

Her gaze connected with Mac as what-if situations bombarded her. "If something happens to me, who will take care of Sugar?"

Mac stepped closer and tilted his head. "There's no way they're going to think that you did this. I don't care what the evidence suggests."

Tali hardly heard him. The little bit she did hear, she didn't believe.

Her gaze remained locked with his. "Will *you* take care of Sugar for me? I can't stand the thought of him going to the pound or . . . something even worse happening to him."

"Tali . . ." he pleaded.

She glanced at everything around her as panic built inside her. "I need to figure out who can take over the store. I still have bills to pay. If I'm in prison, there's no way I'll be able to do that. I have enough savings to cover things for a while. But if the police really think I murdered Donna, then I'll be going away for a long time. I'll lose everything."

Mac touched her arm. "Tali."

Her gaze flung up to meet his, his touch seeming to snap her out of her stupor.

"You need to calm down," he murmured. "I know

that's not what you want to hear. But we're going to get through this."

She shook her head, knowing that nothing he said right now would calm her.

No, her entire future was on the line right now.

And she felt helpless to do anything about it.

Mac stayed with Tali another hour.

He'd fixed her something to drink. Taken Sugar for a walk. Then Tali had said she wanted to rest.

Before she'd done that, she called Cadence to see if her friend might come stay with her.

The girl—she was in her twenties, but still a girl to Mac—had arrived a few minutes later. That's when Mac left.

Part of him wanted to stay. Wanted to try and comfort Tali. He'd seen the distress on her face, and he couldn't blame her for being anxious.

Without saying anything, he instinctively knew that what had happened with her husband was playing into her fears.

His heart hurt for her.

He left her place and headed right to the police station. He wanted to talk to Cassidy himself.

She was in her office when he arrived, and she invited him inside.

He closed the door behind him before sitting across from her desk. This was a place he often visited. Many times, the two of them just chatted about things going on in town. About their personal lives. About Cassidy's baby daughter, Faith.

But, right now, something much more serious hung in the air.

Before Mac could say anything, Cassidy said, "I'm just doing my job, Mac."

Of course, she'd known why he was here.

The last thing Mac wanted was for Cassidy to feel like he was attacking her or questioning her decisions. She had to make hard calls as Chief of Police. Doing the right thing didn't always—or usually, for that matter—mean doing the easy thing.

That was especially true on a small island like this where everyone knew each other.

He shifted in his seat. "I know you are. And I know that requires doing things that you don't always want to do. I'm not here to blame you."

"Then what's on your mind?" She leaned back in her seat, caution still in her gaze.

"I put Tali's husband behind bars thirty years ago." Mac hadn't talked to anyone about this, but it was time.

He needed some wise counsel to know how to handle it. And since Cassidy was a woman, he was interested in hearing her viewpoint.

Cassidy's eyebrows shot up. "What?"

Mac nodded.

He told her about when he'd been working undercover in Atlanta after a string of armed robberies occurred at area banks. Told Cassidy about how the team assigned to the case had discovered an inside man working at the banks who was helping these robbers with their plan. Told her how the only man linked between the banks and the robbers was Jimmy Robinson.

Mac had helped secure evidence leading to the man's arrest. He'd later been found guilty in court. He went to prison to serve a thirty-year sentence and had died from a heart attack before getting parole.

He hadn't realized until Tali told him about her marriage that he knew her husband. That Mac had been the one to help put him behind bars. That he'd been the one who changed Tali's life forever.

She'd been faithful to Jimmy in prison. Never filed for divorce. As a result, she'd never been able to have the family she'd always wanted.

She'd made the best of things, but . . .

"Wow," Cassidy said, her eyebrows still raised with surprise. "I had no idea."

"It's not something I really enjoy talking about."

"I can see why." Cassidy leaned forward, her elbows on her desk. "Mac, it's clear to me that you really care about Tali."

He knew there was no reason to deny it. "I do."

"Have you and Tali talked about it?"

He shrugged. "Just a little. She doesn't seem interested in resurrecting the bad memories."

"I can understand that . . . but don't give up. You'd be surprised at the chasms that can be crossed. It's not always easy to build the bridge. It's not always fast. But it's possible. And love is always worth the risk."

"You sound like you know."

She cast him a weary look. "You know I do."

Yes, he did.

He stored her advice away in the back of his mind.

Because Cassidy was absolutely right.

CHAPTER
TWELVE

TALI SPENT much of the rest of the day in bed.

It wasn't like her to curl up in a ball like this. She was usually a take-life-by-the-horns kind of gal. People admired her ability to let things roll off her back.

Right now, she felt as if she had some sort of mild PTSD. She couldn't stop thinking about that terrible day that Jimmy had been arrested.

The two of them had been sitting at the kitchen table one morning drinking coffee and eating ham and cheese omelets Jimmy had prepared. He only cooked on special occasions. But he'd awoken in an especially good mood and with a new bounce to his step.

He hadn't explained why, had only said things were looking up.

He'd been so handsome with his thick blond hair, square face, and blue eyes. And he was whip smart.

From the first moment they'd met at a friend's party, they'd hit it off and had been inseparable afterward.

Vacation pamphlets were spread on the table in front of them.

Jimmy had just gotten a bonus at work, so they were planning a trip to Hawaii.

Then, after they got home, they'd decided they would try to start a family.

Everything about the conversation and about their future had seemed perfect at that point.

Then someone had knocked at the door.

Jimmy's face had instantly changed. He'd risen, muttering, "I wonder who could be here this early on a Saturday morning . . ."

As soon as he'd opened the door, the police had flooded inside.

They'd arrested Jimmy.

And Tali's life had forever been turned upside down.

Back in the present, Tali tried to focus on Donna's death rather than the life she'd had stolen from her.

Cadence had stayed with her for several hours, but Tali had encouraged her to go home at nine. It was supposed to storm again tonight. She'd heard the weather forecast earlier, and she didn't want Cadence to get caught in it.

The wind was picking up outside. When the storms came from the east, the winds always blew the sand from the beach against her windows, and sand pelted the windows now.

Tali usually enjoyed storms, but tonight she knew she wouldn't.

Not only had she slept too much this evening, but she had too much on her mind to rest.

Instead, she sat on the couch with Sugar, stroking her dog's head as she pondered her future and her past.

As she did, a noise next door caught her ear.

Was that a shout?

Was Tank okay?

Tali froze, still listening.

That's when she heard another yell followed by a crash.

No, things definitely weren't okay.

Tali grabbed a sweater and threw it on.

Before rushing down the steps, she turned toward Sugar. "Stay here, boy. I'll be right back."

By the time she got outside, the storm had strengthened. It was more than wind.

Rain pounded everything within sight. And this wasn't a summer rain. It was a cold, chilling rain that seeped through her clothing all the way to her bones.

Tali reached the door to the surf shop and paused.

It was open.

Why would Tank leave his door open? It was midnight!

She hesitated near the open door.

Especially when she remembered Donna.

That's when Tali decided to call the police. She quickly explained things to the dispatcher, who promised to send someone out.

As Tali heard a loud moan, she feared Tank might need help. Maybe a crime hadn't occurred. What if Tank had an accident and was injured?

Tali shoved aside her concerns about herself and barged into the shop.

She'd been here several times before, so she knew how to find the door to his apartment. She skirted around the checkout counter and into the office at the back of the building.

Turning right, she found the stairway.

The door there was also open and unlocked.

She flipped on the light switch and hurried up the stairs.

When she got to the top, she spotted Tank lying

on the floor just inside his apartment. A phone was in his hands, and blood drizzled from his forehead.

She sank to her knees when she saw him. "Tank . . ."

When he looked at her, his eyes filled with something.

Was that . . . fear?

"Tank, it's just me. Tali."

Before she could ask him any questions, footsteps sounded on the stairway.

When she turned, officers flooded past her to check on Tank followed by EMTs.

Then she saw Cassidy approaching, her expression stony and unyielding.

"Talitha Robinson, I'm afraid you're going to have to come with me."

Tali rose, confused about the police chief's words and abrupt actions. "Come with you?"

Cassidy took her arm. "Tank called 911. We know you attacked him. Now we're going to need to take you in."

Shock coursed through Tali as she sat alone in the interrogation room at the police station.

How had this happened? It didn't make any sense.

She tried to get her breathing under control, tried to keep herself calm. But it was difficult, to say the least.

All she could think about was worst-case scenarios—so much that she nearly felt stiff with fear.

She needed to talk to someone. To tell her side of the story.

How long had Tali been in this room?

It seemed like hours. But in reality, probably only twenty minutes had passed.

Finally, Cassidy came back inside.

"I didn't do this, and I don't understand why you think I did," Tali started before Cassidy could even say anything. "I heard something happening at Tank's place, so I rushed over to make sure he was okay. I even called the police. You can check your records."

"I already did." Cassidy calmly lowered herself into the chair across from her. "There's a record of your call. But Tali . . . Tank identified you as his assailant. He said you're the one who attacked him."

"But I didn't. That's just not possible. He must be confused or something."

Cassidy studied her. "Do you have anyone who can verify your alibi?"

"No, I was alone. Cadence stayed with me until about nine p.m., and then I sent her home. It was just me and Sugar after that."

Cassidy tilted her head. "You have to understand how this looks."

Tali did. It looked bad. *Really* bad. "What exactly did Tank say?"

"Without hesitation, he said it was you."

"He's that certain?" It just didn't make sense. "Are you sure his head injury isn't affecting his memory?"

"He had the lights out watching TV when he heard someone come into his living room. Then he looked up and saw you out of the corner of his eye. He started to get up, but the next thing he knew, something hit him on the head."

No . . . there had to be another explanation.

Tali's mind raced until an idea hit her. "Cassidy . . . what if this killer is just someone who looks like me?"

"I thought of that, and I've been keeping my eyes open. I haven't seen anyone else here who really fits your description. You're almost seventy, you're still active, and you even have great hair. It's not like I run into people your age who look like you every day."

Tali leaned back in her chair, trying to fight despair.

But despair was winning.

Wouldn't it be poetic if both she and Jimmy went to prison for crimes they didn't commit?

CHAPTER
THIRTEEN

WHEN MAC GOT into the office the next morning, the first thing he heard about was Tali's arrest.

Concern rushed through him.

Why hadn't she called him?

But he knew. He knew about the bad memories that came to Tali every time she looked at him.

Yet he wanted to be there. To hear directly from her what had happened.

He was nearly seventy years old. He felt too old to be pining over someone like this. He'd never been into drama, even when he was younger.

Well, maybe he'd been into his own kind of drama, the humorous kind that entertained people. But never emotional or relational drama.

He hardly knew what to do with these feelings.

He gave his secretary a few tasks, and then he headed to the police station. He hoped Cassidy would let him talk to Tali.

Cassidy was walking out the front door when he arrived.

"I wondered how long it would take for you to show up." She crossed her arms and settled in to talk.

"I can't believe you didn't call me."

"It wasn't my call to make." She lowered her voice. "It was Tali's."

An ache throbbed inside Mac at Cassidy's words, but he knew they were true. "How is she?"

"She's shaken, as you can imagine."

"She spent the night here?"

"She did."

He didn't like the thought of it. "Can I see her?"

"That's up to Tali."

This time, Mac crossed his arms. "Could you ask her?"

"Let's head back inside for a moment. Then I have to take Faith to her doctor's appointment."

"Is something wrong?"

"No, it's just for her checkup. Everything is fine."

Relief filled him. He thought of that little girl as his own grandchild. "That's good to hear."

"Come on." Cassidy nodded toward the door. "Let's see what I can do for you."

Tali sagged as she sat in the chair of the interrogation room.

She'd spent the night locked in a jail cell.

A *jail* cell.

Being there had given her a glimpse of what Jimmy had lived through, and her heart ached even more for her deceased husband.

Currently, she'd been brought back into an interrogation room. She'd also called a lawyer, but he couldn't get here until the ferry started running again. When she went to her arraignment later, her lawyer would talk to the judge via Zoom.

It wasn't ideal, but at least it was something.

Tali's entire body ached after sleeping on the thin, stiff cot in the jail cell. Well, she hadn't really slept. But she'd lain there.

Usually, Tali felt like a twenty-five-year-old in a sixty-eight-year-old's body. Her mom used to say that it wasn't until someone had a health crisis that they really started to feel their age.

Apparently, a life crisis could make you feel the same way.

As the door to the interrogation room opened, Tali glanced up.

She'd been hoping that Cassidy would return with good news.

But to her surprise, Cassidy and Mac stood there.

"Mac?" She didn't want to feel relieved to see him, yet part of her did. He always seemed to have such a handle on things.

"I hope you don't mind me coming." He stepped closer, his eyes hooded with worry.

"No, not at all. I'm glad you're here. I just didn't want to disturb you any more than I already have." She'd thought about calling him.

But shock seemed to slow down her reaction times and make her resigned instead.

"You're never a disturbance." His voice sounded low and sincere.

A zing of nerves fluttered through Tali when she realized how concerned Mac sounded.

"I'll leave you two to talk." Cassidy started to close the door.

"Wait!" Tali had thought of something she meant to ask Cassidy earlier.

Cassidy paused.

"What about Ed Hauser?"

"I talked to him. He said he didn't know Donna was on the island, and I'm inclined to believe him.

He doesn't have a record. However, he also doesn't have an alibi."

"Has Tali officially been charged?" Mac asked.

Cassidy frowned. "She has been. She has a bail hearing in an hour." She glanced at Tali. "You can talk to Mac until then."

CHAPTER
FOURTEEN

AS MAC DROVE Tali back to her place after she paid her bail, he felt her nerves.

She didn't look or act like herself. She usually had an easy laugh and sparkling eyes. Right now, she seemed stiff and pale.

What he wouldn't do to be able to take that burden from her and carry it for her.

He parked in a lot close to her place and then walked her to her door. Thankfully, the sun was out today, and the storm was now spinning farther up the coast. A chilly wind remained in its wake.

The good news was that the ferry was supposed to reopen tomorrow morning. Anyone trapped on the island could leave then.

But what if one of those people who were trapped was the killer?

That meant they might be losing their chance to question whoever was guilty.

In other words—time was running out.

As they approached Beach Bound Books and Beans, he spotted someone knocking at Tali's door.

Aubrey.

The woman's face lit when she turned and spotted them.

"Oh, good. I was hoping you'd be home, Tali." Aubrey handed her a casserole dish. "I made you some shepherd's pie. I figured you might not feel like cooking after everything that's happened."

Tali took the dish from her. "Thank you. That's very kind of you."

Aubrey looked her up and down. "You're not looking very good."

Tali looked at her rumpled clothes. "It was a long night."

Aubrey barely seemed to hear her as she turned to Mac. "And I'm glad I ran into you, Mac."

"Why is that?"

"Because you left this at my place last week." She pulled a screwdriver from her purse and handed it to him.

Curiosity filled Tali's gaze, but she looked away as if she didn't want him to see.

He'd only gone to Aubrey's place because she needed help with her water heater.

Was Tali jealous?

If so, he wouldn't delight in her jealousy, but there *was* something about it that gave him a thrill. Maybe the woman did have feelings for him.

"By the way, I know this is none of my business." Aubrey lowered her voice. "But I heard the new girl working next door—"

"Peggy?" Tali asked.

"Yes, she's the one." She touched her finger to the air as if she was Tinkerbell. "I heard she has a criminal history—one that includes breaking and entering."

Mac's breath caught.

Was that right?

That was definitely something worth looking into.

They talked for several more minutes before Aubrey said goodbye and continued down the boardwalk.

Tali reached for her door handle and frowned. "I left this unlocked. I guess that's not a surprise since I rushed out so quickly . . ."

She stepped inside and turned, as if ready to say goodbye to Mac.

"Are you certain you didn't lock the door?" Mac's cop instincts rose, and he pushed past her.

That was when something on Tali's coffee counter caught his eye.

Another stack of books—one that hadn't been there before.

Mac examined the books.

Book Lovers by Emily Henry.

The Reckoning by John Grisham.

The Last Thing He Told Me by Laura Dave.

Before I Called You Mine by Nicole Deese.

When to Walk Away by Gary Thomas.

Never Say Never by Lisa Wingate.

A plastic, old-fashioned-style circular black bomb lay beside it. It was clearly a fake—and clearly left to send a message—a threat.

Tali ran a hand through her hair. "Donna's killer must've come in and left these."

"Someone's clearly trying to send you a message, and I don't like it."

"Me neither . . ." Tali muttered. "It's clearly directed at me . . . and everyone connected to me who loves books, apparently. But what could this mean? The last thing he told me? Leave the world behind? Is this person planning something else? I'm surprised one of the books doesn't have something about being framed in the title."

"Tali . . . We need to check your security camera footage."

Her eyes widened. "Of course!"

She pulled it up on her phone and scrolled through to after midnight when she'd left the place. She fast-forwarded it as she watched herself rushing outside. Not long after, she saw the police hurry toward Tank's.

Her hand covered her mouth as if she was trying to conceal her frown.

Then she slowed the footage when she saw another figure approaching the door.

It was around two a.m., right after all the police had left.

Mac held his breath as he watched.

A woman appeared on the screen. Wearing all black, including a hoodie that was pulled over her face.

The wind blew and pushed the hood away from her face, revealing long blonde hair.

Hair that looked like Tali's.

Mac's heart thrummed harder.

The woman had a bundle of something in her hands. She glanced around before quickly slipping inside. Not even two minutes later, she departed, and ran down the boardwalk.

Who was that woman?

And exactly what was she doing?

Mac wanted to assume she was the one who left the books. But he knew making the wrong assumptions would only lead to more trouble.

CHAPTER
FIFTEEN

TALI WATCHED as Mac sent the video to Cassidy.

She knew the clue probably wouldn't get her very far since all the evidence was stacked against her. But at least it was *something*.

After the phone *whooshed*, the sound indicating the video had been sent, Tali turned to Mac as they stood near a bookshelf in her shop.

"Thank you for everything you've done." Her voice wavered with emotion. He truly had been a godsend.

"Of course. I just want to do more. I'm going to keep asking questions."

She nodded. "But I know right now you need to get back to work."

"Do you need anything before I go?"

"Did you and Aubrey used to date?" Tali sucked

in a breath. She hadn't meant to ask the question. But she couldn't stop thinking about it.

"Aubrey?" He shook his head. "No. I think she'd like to, but I'm not interested."

"Why not?" Tali had already opened up the door to this conversation, so she might as well walk through it.

"Her husband spoiled her." He shrugged. "I suppose husbands are supposed to spoil their wives. But it's different with Aubrey. She likes what she likes, and she wants what she wants. Our lives just wouldn't mesh. She seems the type to use people for her gain . . . among other things. She does like to ask me to help her with home repairs sometimes."

"Good to know."

"There's nothing—" Before he could finish the statement his phone beeped, and he frowned.

He almost sounded resigned—but definitely hesitant. "There's an emergency meeting about our budget. This storm has kicked up some extra repair costs on our streets here in town, and I've got to go give my approval."

"Then go. I'll be fine."

Mac eyed her. "Are you sure?"

She nodded. "I'm positive."

After another hesitant glance, he stepped toward the door. "I'll stop by to check on you later. If you need anything in the meantime, I'm just a phone call away."

She leaned on the door, feeling like she couldn't keep herself upright from all the stress. "Thank you. I appreciate that."

He gave her another lingering glance before going back to his truck.

Once Tali closed and locked the door, she stood there a moment, wondering what to do.

But she didn't have to wonder for long.

Serena showed up with Sugar in her arms.

Tali took the wiggling canine from her and felt herself relax slightly as the dog licked her chin. "Thank you for taking care of the dog for me."

Tali had asked Cassidy to contact Serena about dog sitting, and the girl had agreed.

Tali expected some type of glib remark or offhanded comment from the girl.

But, to Tali's surprise, Serena threw her arms around her and pulled her into a long hug.

"I can't believe this is happening," Serena whispered into her ear, still embracing Tali. "I know you'd never do something like this."

It felt good to hear Serena say those words.

People on this island didn't know Tali that well yet. She hadn't been here that long. Sometimes small, tight-knit communities didn't like outsiders.

Not that Tali had gotten that impression here. But it *was* a possibility. If anyone was going to be guilty, wouldn't people rather it be someone who wasn't quite one of their own?

Serena pulled away, appearing sincerely concerned.

"I'm going to help you figure out who really did this." Serena planted her fists on her hips. "I've been waiting for you to ask for my help. But now it's clear that I cannot wait any longer."

"Serena . . ." Tali appreciated the girl's intentions. But if Mac and Cassidy couldn't figure this out, what made Serena think that she could?

Serena pulled out a notebook from her oversized bag. "I've been making a list of everyone I think could be considered a suspect as well as their possible motive, means, or opportunity. Now, I think we should talk to them. We have no time to lose."

Tali glanced at the list and frowned.

Italian lady. That would be Gia, Tali mused.

Mousy bookworm. That would be Alice.

Lousy ex-boyfriend. Ed Hauser.

Surfer girl next door. Peggy.

Wait . . . Peggy? Aubrey had mentioned her also.

"Why the surfer girl next door?" Tali asked. "Her name is Peggy, by the way."

Serena shrugged. "She's in with some of the surfers on the island. They do drugs."

"Not every surfer or beach bum is a druggie," Tali reminded her.

"I know. But the group Peggy's hanging out with is." Serena shrugged as if it were a foregone conclusion. "I'm wondering if Peggy saw something, Donna confronted her, and then Peggy set you up to take the fall."

"That . . ." Tali shook her head as she tried to find the words. "I don't even know what to say about that."

"It's a definite possibility, right? It would give her motive. Peggy lives close, so she has opportunity. She looks strong so she has the means. Plus, who's to say she wasn't the one who hit Tank in his apartment? She has blonde hair, and if it was nighttime . . ." Serena twisted her head as she let the question hang out there.

"I don't know . . ." Tali thought the theory was a stretch.

She hadn't considered Peggy yet, but she was going to need some time to chew on that theory.

Serena pointed to another person near the top of the list. "However, I'd really like to focus on Alice. She's one of the few people here on this island who knew Donna. She should be the first person we investigate. Plus, she's still here since the ferry isn't reopening until tomorrow. That means if we want to talk to her, then we need to go now."

"I don't want to alienate a colleague."

Serena's gaze locked with hers. "You'd rather go to jail than hurt someone's feelings?"

Tali swallowed hard, the words practically a smack in the face. "When you put it like that . . . let's go talk to Alice."

Just as Tali and Serena stepped outside, so did Tank.

He physically withdrew as soon as he saw Tali.

A bandage covered his forehead from his injury last night.

Guilt washed through Tali, even though she knew she wasn't responsible.

"It wasn't me." Her voice cracked with emotion. "I know what you said you saw, but it wasn't me. I'd never do something like that to you."

Tank's gaze remained guarded. "I just don't know what's going on. Nothing makes sense anymore."

Peggy's image flashed through Tali's mind. Could the woman really be a suspect?

She needed to keep Tank's new employee in the back of her mind.

"I'm going to figure out who did this to you," Tali said. "I promise."

He nodded and then waved goodbye before stepping back into the shop and locking the door.

Tali didn't miss the small discrete action.

He was scared of her.

A strapping, fit thirty-year-old man was scared of a sixty-eight-year-old woman.

Of all things . . .

If Tali was convicted of this crime, she could only imagine what the *Dateline* special on it would look like.

Her smile quickly faded.

It really wasn't funny, mostly because it was too close to reality.

"I'm driving." Serena led Tali to Elsa, her ice cream truck, which was parked in a nearby lot.

Tali paused before climbing in. "Really?"

"Think of it like this. No one's going to think twice about seeing an ice cream truck cruising up and down the road. It's the perfect way to investigate. Believe me."

Tali shrugged, too tired to argue. "If you insist."

She climbed into the passenger seat of the truck, still feeling uneasy.

"You do know Cassidy started off here as an ice

cream truck driver, right?" Serena offered as she put the truck in Drive.

Tali's eyebrows knit together, certain she hadn't heard correctly. "What?"

Serena nodded matter-of-factly. "It's true. I don't know all the details, I just know that's what she did when she first came to the island. Somehow that morphed into her being police chief."

Tali wasn't sure if that made her feel better. But Mac seemed to have a lot of faith and trust in the woman. There had to be more to that story.

Maybe one day Tali would learn more of those details.

Right now, they needed to talk to Alice . . . even if it was a last-ditch effort to find answers.

CHAPTER
SIXTEEN

TALI AND SERENA pulled up to Alice's cousin's place, a little beach box cottage set off from the road by a rather long driveway. Cedar shingles covered the one-story structure, and an old deck stretched around three sides.

"What's Alice like?" Serena stared at the place from her position on the side of the road.

Tali sighed. "I honestly don't know her that well. We've only met in person a couple of times. But she seems like the best kind of introvert—smart, fun, and very pleasant. Not like a killer."

"Well, you don't seem like a killer either. Unfortunately, neither did Ted Bundy."

Her statement didn't make Tali feel better. "I guess appearances can be deceiving."

"Kind of like a horrible book with a great cover, right?"

"I guess so."

They stared at the house before climbing from the truck and starting toward it.

Tali noticed that the trashcan at the end of the driveway had fallen over. Many on the street had, probably because of the strong winds coming from the ocean. It was something she'd seen quite often since she'd moved to the island. It was practically a weekly exercise to pick up trash from fallen cans up and down the side of the road.

But as Tali went to set up the big plastic bin, something inside caught her eye.

"Serena . . . are you seeing what I'm seeing?"

"I don't know. What are you seeing?"

Tali pointed inside the trashcan.

That's where a blonde wig that appeared similar to Tali's actual hair lay twisted among banana peels and water bottles.

"That's definitely not a coincidence." Serena stared into the can and shook her head. "It's evidence."

Alice popped out the front door, craning her neck to see them. As she seemed to recognize Tali, she pulled her oversized sweater across her chest and crept down the steps. When she got closer, Tali saw the knot of confusion between her eyes.

Tali glanced at the woman, trying to figure out if the demure bookstore owner could be behind this.

And not only that, but why?

Tali and Serena both stared at her as she approached.

"What's going on out here? I thought I heard something, so I looked outside and saw you two digging through my cousin's trash." A knot twisted between Alice's brows as she stared back and forth between them.

"We weren't digging through the trash. I was just setting up your cousin's can. That's when I found this." Tali reached into her pocket and grabbed a pen. Using the writing device, she lifted the wig from the trashcan and held it in the air.

Alice's eyes widened. "What's that?"

"That's what we want you to tell us," Serena said. "What's this wig doing here? Did you kill Donna?"

Tali would have never been that direct and blunt. But maybe it was a good thing Serena was here so they could get to the heart of the matter.

Alice gasped, and her hand went over her heart. "How could you say such a thing? I would never do something like that."

"Are you sure you didn't dress up like Tali and sneak into her store in the middle of the night to end some type of secret feud you and Donna had?" Serena stared at the woman, her gaze unblinking and her stature almost intimidating.

"No!" Alice said. "I wouldn't do that. And the two of us didn't have any type of feud."

"That's not what I heard." Serena crossed her arms, her voice sounding airy and confident.

Tali stared at the girl a moment. Had Serena really heard something like that? Or was she bluffing?

"I don't know what's going on here." Alice threw her hands in the air as her voice tightened. "All I want is to get home. And now you're accusing me of a crime? I heard that you were the one who did it, Tali. Are you just trying to point a finger at someone else to get the attention off yourself? Life isn't always like a mystery novel, you know. Sometimes, the answers are simple and obvious."

Tali cleared her throat, knowing Alice was correct. "I don't want to throw out any false accusations either. We just came here to talk, to see if you knew anything. Then we found this evidence. I can't ignore it, Alice. If I'm charged with this murder, I'm going away for the rest of my life."

"And if *I'm* charged with this crime then I'll go

away for the rest of *my* life." Alice shoved her thumb into her own chest to emphasize each of her words.

The two women stared at each other.

Tali tried to read Alice's body language, tried to get a feel for if she was telling the truth or not.

But, right now, she had no idea.

CHAPTER
SEVENTEEN

"I DIDN'T DO THIS, TALI." Alice stared at her, her gaze unwavering. "If it makes you feel better, I don't believe you killed Donna either. I think someone is setting you up."

"I appreciate that." Tali felt her shoulders relax slightly. "And honestly, I can't imagine you being guilty. Not Gia either. I mean, why would *anyone* want to kill Donna?"

Alice rubbed her arms. "I can't stop thinking about what happened. I'm sorry. I guess I owe you an apology. I've been trying to distance myself from you since this happened. But I should have been there for you. I guess it's just that I only like my drama in books."

"Me too." A cool breeze blew across the water, leaving Tali chilled.

"This is a beautiful moment." Serena sounded impatient. "But we have to find a killer. I think I might have an idea on how to draw this person out."

Tali turned to her, curious to know what the girl would say.

Since Alice wasn't a suspect in her mind, Tali didn't mind if she stayed.

"A lot of people are worried about you, Tali," Serena said. "I think we should call them all together under the guise of helping you out. Then we should ask pointed questions until someone comes forward or slips up—kind of like that ending scene in *Knives Out*."

Tali squirmed inside. "Do you really think that would work?"

Serena's eyes glimmered with satisfaction as she nodded.

"I really do." Then Serena glanced at Alice. "But we're going to have to give this wig to Cassidy, especially if there's DNA evidence on it."

Alice frowned as if she didn't like that idea, but she finally shrugged. "You won't find mine on it. So go ahead."

"You're going to do *what*?" Mac stared at Serena.

Serena had parked her ice cream truck in front of city hall and blared "Mr. Policeman" by Brad Paisley.

It had only taken a couple of minutes for Mac to hear the commotion and come out.

He stood by the passenger-side window, peering inside and scowling at Serena.

Thankfully, it wasn't raining right now.

Serena and her shenanigans . . . he mentally shook his head in exhaustion.

"We're going to draw the killer out," Serena repeated. "I just dropped Tali off at her store so she could get ready for it."

"That sounds like a *terrible* idea."

"Well, thank you." Her eyes glimmered as if that were a compliment.

Mac continued to stare at her, wondering if Serena had even heard what he said. Because she seemed unfazed. Then again, that was par for the course when it came to Serena.

"Anyway, be at the bookstore tonight," Serena continued. "At six. You're not going to want to miss this."

"Serena . . ." His voice held warning.

She put her truck into Drive but paused before going anywhere. "Yes?"

"I don't think you know what you're doing. You're in over your head."

"Maybe. That's why we need you there. But even more, I think *Tali* needs you there. I see the way you two look at each other. You've got a thing for her, and she's got a thing for you too."

Mac let out a breath.

He didn't even know how to respond.

Thankfully, Serena pulled away, putting him out of his misery.

He reflected on the plan that she had laid out.

The whole scheme sounded crazy. But maybe it would work.

His thoughts went back to the wig.

What if someone was pretending to be Tali in an effort to make her look guilty?

But the thing he didn't understand was why somebody would do that.

Maybe tonight would provide some of those answers.

CHAPTER
EIGHTEEN

TALI'S NERVES raked through her as she waited for people to arrive at her bookstore. She'd set out some drinks and treats—she couldn't seem to help herself from being a polite hostess. Serena had also borrowed some folding chairs from someone and had set them up in the center of the space, almost as if they were having a town meeting.

Every time Tali stared at the center of the floor, all she could imagine was Donna's dead body. Maybe it was a good thing the chairs covered that area now.

As she began to absently straighten some of the sugar packets she'd set out, she came to a stop at a stack of books left on an end table.

Her breath caught as she read the titles there.

I See You by Mary Burton.

Blood, Sweat, and Tea by Tom Reynolds.

Anxious People by Fredrik Backman.

After We Say Goodbye by Tammy Gray.

Conviction by Denise Mina.

Tali's heart pounded harder.

Had the killer been in here again?

"Don't worry," someone said behind her.

Tali startled as she turned around.

Serena stood there. Of course.

She was the only other person here right now.

"I did that," Serena explained.

"You did *this*?" Tali pointed to the stack of books.

"That's right. I want the killer to see the book spine poetry and feel a little freaked out."

Tali wasn't sure whether she should be impressed or shake the girl.

She didn't have a chance to do either.

Instead, she attempted a smile as the first attendees arrived: Cadence and Abby. They both gave her a hug and promised her everything would be okay.

It was such an easy promise to make and a hard one to keep. But everyone said it with the best intentions. Even Tali often spoke those words.

In some way or another, everything *would* be okay. Maybe not how Tali wanted it. But there was a silver lining to every cloud if you looked for it. Even if she went to prison, good could come from that bad.

But that still wasn't what she wanted.

"Can I talk to you a minute?" Gia asked as soon as she arrived.

"Sure . . . but more people are coming soon."

"I know. I won't be long."

They walked to a corner to chat. Tali's nerves buzzed with anticipation.

"Listen, I know you're suspicious of me," Gia started. "And it's true that Donna and I did have a disagreement. But I wouldn't have killed her over it!"

Tali waited, feeling as if Gia had more to say. "Good to know."

"*That's* why I said I shouldn't have come here," Gia said. "I didn't really enjoy being around Donna. She's not exactly the life of the party. In fact, she always looked so dour that she was a real buzz kill."

Tali didn't want to agree with Gia, but she could see her point.

But she had other questions. "Thanks for sharing that. Why did you look so sleepy the morning after Donna died?"

"The storm really did keep me up. And I wondered if Donna was up to something again."

"What do you mean?" Tali wasn't sure she liked where this was going.

"I think I know what *calibrate* means."

Tali's pulse quickened. "Please share."

"I talked about doing a scavenger hunt for Halloween that would be a bit of a murder mystery. Certain clues would be put in certain books. The clues were words that you put together to solve a riddle."

"And you think Donna wanted to do something like that also?"

Gia frowned and nodded. "It's just a guess. I wanted to believe she was copying me. But I called Jeannine myself. She told me that Donna likes this blogger I also follow. All of it might be a coincidence, but . . ."

"So why would she give me the word calibrate?"

"My guess is that she wanted to pique your interest, that she was going to run the idea by you in the morning. She just never had the chance."

Tali watched as more people filed into the bookstore. It was going to be jam-packed tonight, and she felt honored that so many people in town would come to support her.

Peggy and Tank showed up. The man still looked nervous, but at least he was here.

Some of the contractors she'd used—including Austin Brooks and Wes O'Neill as well as their wives

—came, as did Lisa and Braden Dillinger, Serena's boyfriend, Webster, and a few Blackout members. Doc Clemson and his girlfriend, Ernestine, came, and even Cassidy had shown up, looking casual in jeans and a knit top.

Tali's eyes widened when Ed Hauser stepped inside also.

If many more people came, there would be standing room only.

Tali's gaze searched the crowd.

Where was Mac?

And why did it mean so much to her that he come?

Tali wasn't sure.

She straightened her beige jumper, an outfit the book club girls had helped pick out for her, along with a long necklace with a seashell at the end.

The girls—Serena, specifically—had gone on and on about dressing for the part. Whatever Tali did, she couldn't look like a vixen.

Like Tali *ever* looked like a vixen.

But she'd gone along with it.

The last group to arrive were the ladies from the widows' group at Tali's church.

She greeted each one, keeping her voice solemn. This was no occasion to be perky.

Finally, Mac stepped inside.

His gaze instantly went to her, and Tali felt relief wash through her.

It was time this meeting got started.

CHAPTER
NINETEEN

MAC WANTED to stand beside Tali. But he wasn't sure the action would be welcome.

Besides, the room was crowded. And she was on the other side, surrounded by members of her book club.

Before he could think about it for too long, Serena stepped to the front of the room and clicked her spoon against a glass. She did it a few times too many until his eardrums ached. Apparently, others felt the same way as their hands covered the sides of their heads.

"Thank you all for coming here," Serena started. She'd dressed in slacks, a button-up shirt, and suspenders.

Mac couldn't be sure, but was she trying to look like that detective from *Knives Out*?

When he'd first met the girl, she'd been fond of dressing as a different character every day as she drove her ice cream route. He thought she'd moved beyond that phase, but maybe not.

"As you know, our dear Tali Robinson has been accused of a horrible crime she did not commit," Serena continued. "If you're here tonight, it's because you, like me, want to help prove she's innocent. You know what they always say—two minds are better than one. In this case, I'm going to go with twenty minds are better than one."

Soft chuckles went through the room.

Mac had to hand it to Serena. The girl had charisma and guts.

"What we need to figure out is why somebody would have wanted to murder Donna," Serena continued. "Not why *Tali* would want to murder *Donna* because we all know she *wouldn't*. But the way we're going to find this mysterious blonde killer is by identifying who had a motive for murder."

"You said mysterious blonde killer?" Axel lounged back in his seat, holding his girlfriend's hand and looking casual and maybe even slightly entertained. "Can you elaborate?"

"That's right," Serena said. "I believe someone donned a blonde wig in order to look like Tali and frame her."

Gasps and whispers traveled around the room.

Mac was glad he was one of the last people to arrive. It gave him a good excuse to stand near the front of the room but on the edge. From here, he had a view of everybody and could pick out anyone who acted squirmy.

"Now, I know that most of you in here didn't know Donna," Serena said, a terse expression on her face. "We know Alice, Gia, and Ed knew her. Thank you all for coming because I know this can't be easy for you."

"And Tali," Tank added with a sheepish frown. "I mean, if we're going to get everything out in the open here, then we need to establish that Tali knew Donna also."

Serena scowled before returning to her uptight detective persona. "Point taken. And Tali also knew her, having just met her in person that night."

"I'm not sure how the rest of us can help if we didn't know her," Trixie from the widows' group said. Outspoken Trixie had been married three times and dyed her short hair a bright red color that only emphasized the age spots on her face. But she was a hoot to hang out with.

"I realize that, but I'm hoping that maybe *someone* here saw *something* that could help us."

"Did Donna look anything like Tali?" Austin

asked. "Could someone have mistaken the two women? What if they were trying to kill Tali instead?"

The statement made Mac's heart beat overtime. That was *not* what he'd expected to hear.

But it made sense.

Why hadn't they thought of that earlier?

Everyone turned and studied Tali.

Her cheeks reddened under the scrutiny.

"I don't even think they look similar." Skepticism saturated Serena's voice. "I mean, Tali is so pretty, and Donna was . . ."

She didn't finish the statement. It was probably better that way.

Because Mac knew what she didn't want to say aloud.

Donna had been rather homely and probably twenty pounds heavier.

The two women *did* bear some similarities. It *was* nighttime and hard to see. Especially with the power out.

Maybe someone snuck up on Donna thinking she was Tali.

"I think we need to start by identifying the usual motives for murder." Abby stood to address the crowd, looking as if this was a stage play instead of real life. "I did a murder mystery show back in

Myrtle Beach when I lived there, and that was a very important aspect of the production. Motive, means, and opportunity."

"Mac, what are the three reasons people usually kill?" Serena turned toward him.

He shrugged as everyone's attention turned toward him. "Love, money, and power."

"So let's run with that idea for a minute," Serena said. "Maybe somebody *did* want to kill Tali but accidentally killed Donna. If that's the case, who would that be?"

Everyone's gaze turned to Tali as they waited for her response.

———

Tali inwardly cringed. If there was one thing she hated, it was being the center of attention—especially when she wasn't *trying* to be the center of attention.

She swallowed her embarrassment and tried to think this through. She had to give these people *something* or they were just going to keep staring at her.

"If people kill for love, money, and power, then they wouldn't have tried to kill me because of money or power. That's for sure because I'm nearly broke." Tali let out a withering chuckle. "I hope if I don't go to jail, the bookstore will stay open and that you'll all shop here."

A round of murmurs and even a few laughs traveled through the room.

"So that leaves love." Smugness captured Serena's voice.

Tali felt her cheeks warm again.

Was Serena right? Had someone tried to kill Tali for love?

What sense would that make?

None.

"But I'm single." Tali shrugged and tried to brush the statement off. "So if that's the kind of love they're talking about, I'm out of ideas."

"You haven't had any romantic interests or dated since you arrived in town?" Abby stared across the room at her with a twinkle in her gaze.

Now Tali was *really* hating this. But she didn't dare glance at Mac. She knew the speculation that would cause if she did.

"I mean . . . not really." Tali shrugged again. "I *am* sixty-eight."

"But you're not dead," Doc Clemson said. "You still deserve a chance at love."

He smiled at Ernestine beside him. The two had only found each other a couple of years ago, and now they were two peas in a pod. At least, that's what Mac had told Tali once.

This whole situation was getting worse and worse.

But what if this theory about love and romance was true?

Could this murder somehow tie in with Jimmy?

But why would someone want to kill *Tali* because of *Jimmy*? Unless someone on the island thought they were swindled by Jimmy during one of the bank robberies.

That seemed so far-fetched and unlikely.

That would only leave . . . Mac.

Tali's thoughts raced at that realization.

What if someone killed Donna thinking Donna was Tali?

But the only reason someone might do that was out of jealousy . . . jealousy over . . . Mac? Did that even make sense?

Tali's gaze fell on the only person she'd encountered since arriving on the island who seemed to have strong feelings for Mac.

Aubrey Jones.

The woman sat in her seat with her legs daintily crossed and every hair in place as she listened to the discussion.

A woman as prissy as that would never resort to murder . . . right?

Tali couldn't be sure.

Because just last week, she'd watched a true crime show about Jodi Arias.

It reminded her that a murderer could take on many forms and appearances.

CHAPTER
TWENTY

AS MAC LISTENED to the conversation, his gaze fell on Aubrey.

Was that guilt on her face?

Tension stretched through the air as everyone seemed to turn their gaze toward her.

Did everyone in town know that Aubrey liked Mac?

He wasn't sure how he felt about that. He preferred to keep things like his love life private. However, he didn't even *have* a love life with Aubrey. Just because the woman had been interested did not mean anything was there between them.

Finally, the woman seemed to crack. She uncrossed her legs and glanced around as if realizing everyone was looking to her for answers.

"Why would *I* do this?" Aubrey asked.

"Exactly. Why *would* you kill Donna?" Serena narrowed her eyes at the woman.

"Everyone knows you have a thing for Mac," Ernestine said the statement matter-of-factly.

"So you think I'd kill a stranger?" Aubrey's voice stretched out until it cracked.

"I did see you leave your house in the middle of the night while I was out patrolling," Officer Braden Dillinger said. "I didn't think anything of it at the time. Where were you going?"

Aubrey scowled. "Someone smelled smoke in their home and thought it could be an electrical issue with their heating system, if you must know. Turned out to be nothing."

Cassidy glanced around the room. "Can anyone here verify that?"

"The house didn't belong to anyone in this room," Aubrey snapped. "It was a rental. But, if you insist, I can find the address.

Cassidy continued to stare at her. "Do you always respond to calls yourself? I thought you had employees who did that for you."

"My two workers have the week off. It's October. We usually don't have that many issues at this time of year, and even tradesmen have to take vacations sometime." Her shoulders stiffened again. "What else do you want me to say? I didn't realize I was on trial here."

Mac continued to watch her, his thoughts racing.

Just what was this woman hiding?

Based on Aubrey's body language, she was definitely keeping secrets.

Tali listened closely to the conversation without reservation as she observed Aubrey.

Now that she thought about it, the two of them were the same size—five feet five inches and fairly trim. From a distance, and if Aubrey was wearing a wig, they might look alike.

Tali envisioned Donna a moment—paranoid Donna—hearing something downstairs. If the woman thought there could be danger, she might have grabbed one of the knives from Tali's kitchen and gone to check it out.

But why wouldn't Donna have woken Tali? Unless she liked to handle these things herself. Donna *did* hate having that paranoid reputation.

Tali imagined Donna going downstairs and seeing someone in the shop.

Then that person—Aubrey—spotting her.

Maybe the two women argued, especially when Aubrey realized that Donna had dated Ed. Tali wasn't sure what that argument would've been about, except that one of the women had said, "You should've never come here."

That's what Tank said he heard.

Maybe something snapped in Aubrey when she saw the woman Ed had left her for—especially considering Donna was far less attractive. Had her pride caused bitterness over that fact?

Did that argument somehow lead to murder?

In a strange, twisted way, it made sense.

Tali continued to watch Aubrey, who was growing cagey under the scrutiny of everyone around her.

"Most women don't stab people in the back when they kill them," Aubrey finally said, her voice crisp. "All of you mystery lovers should know that. Women usually kill by poison."

"That's actually a misnomer," Mac said. "Women more often kill with sharp objects or asphyxia whereas men kill with blunt objects or firearms. Women are also more likely to kill in an act of unpremeditated rage, in the victim's home, and they usually know the person who's killed."

Defiance filled Aubrey's gaze. "I don't have to take this!"

Aubrey stood, ready to leave.

But before she could even take a step, Cassidy moved in front of the door. "I don't think you leaving is a good idea right now."

CHAPTER
TWENTY-ONE

MAC DIDN'T LIKE where this was going.

From what he knew about Aubrey, she had an angry streak. One of her sons had her same personality—a real hothead at times.

Aubrey covered it up more. Did she cover it up with passive-aggressiveness?

Maybe.

When Aubrey sat back down, Tali rose.

Her narrowed gaze was on Aubrey. "You broke into my place wearing a wig so you could look like me. You probably wore gloves so you wouldn't leave any prints. You left those books as a threat to me. *Misery? Sweet Revenge? Danger Is Everywhere?*"

Before I Called You Mine and *The Reckoning* suddenly made a little more sense as well.

This was all about a man and unrequited love, wasn't it?

"Did you do all of that because of Mac? Were you afraid that I was moving in on your territory?" Tali stared at her. "If that was your motive, then Donna died in vain. Because Mac and I are just friends, and that's all we'll ever be."

Her words caught Mac by surprise, and an ache jabbed him in his chest.

He pushed the feeling away before anyone could see the rejection in his gaze.

He'd deal with that later.

Aubrey remained silent, not saying anything.

Tali continued. "I'm assuming you wore the wig in case anyone saw you, so they would think that you were me. But I have an alarm, and my door was locked. So how did you get in?"

"She knows how to pick locks." Austin Brooks said the words calmly as if he were talking about choosing a new paint color for a bathroom. "Her dad was a locksmith and taught her. Sometimes she has to do that to get into people's houses and fix their units. That's what I heard from her crew when I was fixing up another house, at least."

"So she must have known the power was out and seized the opportunity," Serena muttered.

"Now, now—we shouldn't be so harsh and judgmental." Trixie nodded gently as her gaze met those of the people around her.

"Thank you, Trixie," Aubrey said.

"Just because Aubrey was obsessed with Mac doesn't mean she would kill for him."

Aubrey's mouth dropped open as if she couldn't believe her friend had said those words. "Trixie . . . !"

"What if she didn't do it on purpose?" Gia suggested, her eyes sparkling with gregariousness. "Maybe it was all an accident, a crime of passion. That happens quite often—at least in those romance novels I love to read."

As people began to discuss crimes of passion—throwing out Aubrey's name—Aubrey stood again and sliced her hands through the air. "Stop it! Stop talking about me as if I'm not here."

Tali continued watching carefully, hardly able to breathe.

What would Aubrey say now?

As silence stretched through the room, Cadence reached over and squeezed Tali's hand as if sensing her nerves.

Tali squeezed back, appreciating the girl's thoughtfulness.

But Tali nearly felt beside herself as she waited for what would happen next.

Aubrey's gaze darted around the room.

She knew that she was cornered with no way out.

Even if she denied it at this point, it would be of no use.

Everyone in this room now thought she was guilty.

"Fine," she finally said. "I did it, okay? I didn't mean to. Donna kept coming at me, and she wouldn't stop. She said she was going to go to the police to turn me in. That I was going to spend the rest of my life in jail."

"For breaking in?" Serena asked.

"Yes, ridiculous, right?" Aubrey shrugged as if embarrassed and then began fanning her face with her hand. "Looking back, I realize she was just being aggressive because we'd both dated Ed. He regretted breaking up with me for her and came to me later, begging me to take him back. Anyway, the whole thing was preposterous."

"You were very upset when I broke up with you to date her," Ed piped in. "You like getting what you want. You can't deny that."

"Don't be absurd." Aubrey turned up her nose. "Donna looked so smug that something snapped inside me. When she turned around to grab her phone, I saw the knife she'd been carrying. I grabbed it. Before I comprehended what I was doing, I plunged it toward her. Then I grasped what I'd done. I realized I'd killed her. And so, I ran."

Tali's heart continued to pound harder.

She couldn't believe what she was hearing.

"If that's true, then why did you attack me?" Tank asked, blinking as if totally baffled. "What sense does *that* make?"

"I knew you might have seen something. I saw you walk past. I needed you to stay quiet. I thought maybe if you felt threatened, you would."

"Then you came back to my shop and left more books?" Tali asked. "Weren't you just setting yourself up to look guilty? You could have been caught!"

"I'm not a trained killer, for the love of Pete! I just needed to keep people quiet. That's all. I didn't want any of this to happen, and I was desperate to resolve the situation." Aubrey raised her chin defiantly. "I have nothing further to say."

Cassidy stepped toward her. "Aubrey Jones, you are under arrest for the death of Donna Winters and the assault on Tank Dietz. You have the right to remain silent . . ."

CHAPTER
TWENTY-TWO

MAC WATCHED as people slowly filed from the storefront.

Most had stopped first to give their condolences or apologies—sometimes both—to Tali for the murder, for the fact she'd been accused of the crime, and for everything she'd been through.

It wasn't the welcome to Lantern Beach that people here on this island usually gave newcomers.

Especially newcomers like Tali.

Her words still remained in Mac's head.

She'd made a public profession that the two of them could never be together.

How much clearer could it be?

Mac needed to end his infatuation with this woman and move on.

But why did he think that was going to be easier said than done?

He shifted awkwardly in front of her as they stood there, and he saw the emotions fluttering through Tali's gaze as she pushed her hair behind her ear.

"Thank you so much for everything you did for me," she started. "It really means so much."

"I'm glad I could help."

She rubbed her throat as if swallowing hard. "Listen, about what I said at the meeting . . ."

"You don't have to explain," he quickly insisted.

"I know I don't *have* to, but I *want* to." Her lips slipped down into a frown. "I didn't intend to say what I did in front of everyone."

"If it's the truth, then there's no reason to hide it."

She shook her head, emotions swirling in her gaze. "This *is* the truth. I do care about you. But every time my feelings for you begin to grow, I remember Jimmy. I don't know how to reconcile my old life with my new one."

"I'm hoping you might be able to forgive me for what happened."

"I'm working on it. I really am. I just need more time." Her voice sounded barely above a whisper.

Mac shifted closer to her. "You can have all the time you want. But I hope one day, when you're ready, that the two of us can sit down and talk about what happened with Jimmy. Maybe that would help things make more sense for you—if you could see my perspective. I realize it's probably not what you want to hear, but it seems like a good idea to get these things out in the open."

Tali stared at him another moment before nodding. "I think that's a good idea also. Let's talk—really talk—sometime."

"Okay." Mac felt a small sense of satisfaction that maybe, at least, they would make some progress.

But now he knew it was time for him to leave.

To his surprise, Tali reached forward and pulled him into a hug.

After his momentary shock wore off, he wrapped his arms around her too and held her close for a moment.

When she pulled away, he saw the gratitude in her gaze. Along with . . . warmth and affection.

Mac regretted that Donna had to die to get him and Tali to this moment. But he was also happy that he and Tali may have finally reached a turning point.

At least, he prayed that was the case.

Murder, disaster, and mystery seemed to have bound them together. But those were also the very things that could pull them apart.

As Mac pushed another stray hair from Tali's face, he prayed that the former would be true.

~~~

Thank you so much for reading *Bound by Mystery*. If you enjoyed this book, please consider leaving a review.

Stay tuned for the next and final book in the Beach Bound Books and Beans series: *Bound by Trouble.*

OTHER BOOKS IN THE LANTERN BEACH SERIES:

LANTERN BEACH MYSTERIES

Hidden Currents

You can take the detective out of the investigation, but you can't take the investigator out of the detective. A notorious gang puts a bounty on Detective Cady Matthews's head after she takes down their leader, leaving her no choice but to hide until she can testify at trial. But her temporary home across the country on a remote North Carolina island isn't as peaceful as she initially thinks. Living under the new identity of Cassidy Livingston, she struggles to keep her investigative skills tucked away, especially after a body washes ashore. When local police bungle the murder investigation, she can't resist stepping in. But Cassidy is supposed to be keeping a low profile. One wrong move could lead to both her discovery and her demise. Can she bring justice to the island . . . or will the hidden currents surrounding her pull her under for good?

Flood Watch

The tide is high, and so is the danger on Lantern Beach. Still in hiding after infiltrating a dangerous gang, Cassidy Livingston just has to make it a few more months before she can testify at trial and resume her old life. But trouble keeps finding her, and Cassidy is pulled into a local investigation after a man mysteriously disappears from the island she now calls home. A recurring nightmare from her time undercover only muddies things, as does a visit from the parents of her handsome ex-Navy SEAL neighbor. When a friend's life is threatened, Cassidy must make choices that put her on the verge of blowing her cover. With a flood watch on her emotions and her life in a tangle, will Cassidy find the truth? Or will her past finally drown her?

Storm Surge

A storm is brewing hundreds of miles away, but its effects are devastating even from afar. Laid-back, loose, and light: that's Cassidy Livingston's new motto. But when a makeshift boat with a bloody cloth inside washes ashore near her oceanfront home, her detective instincts shift into gear . . . again. Seeking clues isn't the only thing on her mind—romance is heating up with next-door neighbor and former Navy SEAL Ty Chambers as well. Her heart wants the love and stability she's longed for her entire life. But her hidden identity only leads to a tidal wave of turbulence. As more answers emerge about the boat, the danger around her rises, creating a treacherous swell that threatens to reveal her past. Can Cassidy mind her own business, or will the storm surge of violence and corruption that has washed ashore on Lantern Beach leave her life in wreckage?

Dangerous Waters

Danger lurks on the horizon, leaving only two choices: find shelter or flee. Cassidy Livingston's new identity has begun to feel as comfortable as her favorite sweater. She's been tucked away on Lantern Beach for weeks, waiting to testify against a deadly gang, and is settling in to a new life she wants to last forever. When she thinks she spots someone malevolent from her past, panic swells inside her. If an enemy has found her, Cassidy won't be the only one who's a target. Everyone she's come to love will also be at risk. Dangerous waters threaten to pull her into an overpowering chasm she may never escape. Can

Cassidy survive what lies ahead? Or has the tide fatally turned against her?

Perilous Riptide

Just when the current seems safer, an unseen danger emerges and threatens to destroy everything. When Cassidy Livingston finds a journal hidden deep in the recesses of her ice cream truck, her curiosity kicks into high gear. Islanders suspect that Elsa, the journal's owner, didn't die accidentally. Her final entry indicates their suspicions might be correct and that what Elsa observed on her final night may have led to her demise. Against the advice of Ty Chambers, her former Navy SEAL boyfriend, Cassidy taps into her detective skills and hunts for answers. But her search only leads to a skeletal body and trouble for both of them. As helplessness threatens to drown her, Cassidy is desperate to turn back time. Can Cassidy find what she needs to navigate the perilous situation? Or will the riptide surrounding her threaten everyone and everything Cassidy loves?

Deadly Undertow

The current's fatal pull is powerful, but so is one detective's will to live. When someone from Cassidy Livingston's past shows up on Lantern Beach and warns her of impending peril, opposing currents collide, threatening to drag her under. Running would be easy. But leaving would break her heart. Cassidy must decipher between the truth and lies, between reality and deception. Even more importantly, she must decide whom to trust and whom to fear. Her life depends on it. As danger rises and answers surface, everything Cassidy thought she knew is tested. In order to survive, Cassidy must take drastic measures and end the battle against the ruthless gang DH-7 once and for all. But if her final mission fails, the consequences will be as deadly as the raging undertow.

LANTERN BEACH ROMANTIC SUSPENSE

Tides of Deception

Change has come to Lantern Beach: a new police chief, a new season, and . . . a new romance? Austin Brooks has loved Skye Lavinia from the moment they met, but the walls she keeps around her seem impenetrable. Skye knows Austin is the best thing to ever happen to her. Yet she also knows that if he learns the truth about her past, he'd be a fool not to run. A chance encounter brings secrets bubbling to the surface, and danger soon follows. Are the life-threatening events plaguing them really accidents . . . or is someone trying to send a deadly message? With the tides on Lantern Beach come deception and lies. One question remains—who will be swept away as the water shifts? And will it bring the end for Austin and Skye, or merely the beginning?

Shadow of Intrigue

For her entire life, Lisa Garth has felt like a supporting character in the drama of life. The designation never bothered her—until now. Lantern Beach, where she's settled and runs a popular restaurant, has boarded up for the season. The slower pace leaves her with too much time alone. Braden Dillinger came to Lantern Beach to try to heal. The former Special Forces officer returned from battle with invisible scars and diminished hope. But his recovery is hampered by the fact that an unknown enemy is trying to kill him. From the moment Lisa and Braden meet, danger ignites around them, and both are drawn into a web of intrigue that turns their lives upside down. As shadows creep in, will Lisa and Braden be able to shine a light on the peril around them? Or will the encroaching darkness turn their worst nightmares into reality?

Storm of Doubt

A pastor who's lost faith in God. A romance

writer who's lost faith in love. A faceless man with a deadly obsession. Nothing has felt right in Pastor Jack Wilson's world since his wife died two years ago. He hoped coming to Lantern Beach might help soothe the ragged edges of his soul. Instead, he feels more alone than ever. Novelist Juliette Grace came to the island to hide away. Though her professional life has never been better, her personal life has imploded. Her husband left her and a stalker's threats have grown more and more dangerous. When Jack saves Juliette from an attack, he sees the terror in her gaze and knows he must protect her. But when danger strikes again, will Jack be able to keep her safe? Or will the approaching storm prove too strong to withstand?

Winds of Danger

Wes O'Neill is perfectly content to hang with his friends and enjoy island life on Lantern Beach. Something begins to change inside him when Paige Henderson sweeps into his life. But the beautiful newcomer is hiding painful secrets beneath her cheerful facade. Police dispatcher Paige Henderson came to Lantern Beach riddled with guilt and uncertainties after the fallout of a bad relationship. When she meets Wes, she begins to open up to the possibility of love again. But there's something Wes isn't telling her—something that could change everything. As the winds shift, doubts seep into Paige's mind. Can Paige and Wes trust each other, even as the currents work against them? Or is trouble from the past too much to overcome?

Rains of Remorse

A stranger invades her home, leaving Rebecca Jarvis terrified. Above all, she must protect the baby growing inside her. Since her estranged husband died suspiciously six months earlier, Rebecca has been determined to depend on no one but herself. Her chivalrous new neighbor appears to be an answer to prayer. But who is Levi Stoneman really? Rebecca wants to believe he can help her, but she can't ignore her instincts. As danger closes in, both Rebecca and Levi must figure out whom they can trust. With Rebecca's baby coming soon, there's no time to waste. Can the truth prevail . . . or will remorse overpower the best of intentions?

Torrents of Fear

The woman lingering in the crowd can't be Allison . . . can she? Because Allison was pronounced dead six years ago. Musician Carter Denver knows only one person who's capable of helping him find answers: Sadie Thompson, his estranged best friend and someone who also knew Allison. He needs to know if he's losing his mind or if Allison could have survived her car accident. Could Allison really be alive? If so, why is she trying to harm Carter and Sadie? As the two try to find answers, can Sadie keep her feelings for Carter hidden? Could he ever care for her, or is the man of her dreams still in love with the woman now causing his nightmares?

LANTERN BEACH PD

On the Lookout

When Cassidy Chambers accepted the job as police chief on Lantern Beach, she knew the island had its secrets. But a suspicious death with potentially far-reaching implications will test all her skills —and threaten to reveal her true identity. Cassidy enlists the help of her husband, former Navy SEAL Ty Chambers. As they dig for answers, both uncover parts of their pasts that are best left buried. Not everything is as it seems, and they must figure out if their John Doe is connected to the secretive group that has moved onto the island. As facts materialize, danger on the island grows. Can Cassidy and Ty discover the truth about the shadowy crimes in their cozy community? Or has darkness permanently invaded their beloved Lantern Beach?

Attempt to Locate

A fun girls' night out turns into a nightmare when armed robbers barge into the store where Cassidy and her friends are shopping. As the situation escalates and the men escape, a massive manhunt launches on Lantern Beach to apprehend the dangerous trio. In the midst of the chaos, a potential foe asks for Cassidy's help. He needs to find his sister who fled from the secretive Gilead's Cove community on the island. But the more Cassidy learns about the seemingly untouchable group, the more her unease grows. The pressure to solve both cases continues to mount. But as the gravity of the situation rises, so does the danger. Cassidy is determined to protect the island and break up the cult . . . but doing so might cost her everything.

First Degree Murder

Police Chief Cassidy Chambers longs for a break from the recent crimes plaguing Lantern Beach. She simply wants to enjoy her friends' upcoming wedding, to prepare for the busy tourist season about to slam the island, and to gather all the dirt she can on the suspicious community that's invaded the town. But trouble explodes on the island, sending residents—including Cassidy—into a squall of uneasiness. Cassidy may have more than one enemy plotting her demise, and the collateral damage seems unthinkable. As the temperature rises, so does the pressure to find answers. Someone is determined that Lantern Beach would be better off without their new police chief. And for Cassidy, one wrong move could mean certain death.

Dead on Arrival

With a highly charged local election consuming the community, Police Chief Cassidy Chambers braces herself for a challenging day of breaking up petty conflicts and tamping down high emotions. But when widespread food poisoning spreads among potential voters across the island, Cassidy smells something rotten in the air. As Cassidy examines every possibility to uncover what's going on, local enigma Anthony Gilead again comes on her radar. The man is running for mayor and his cult-like following is growing at an alarming rate. Cassidy feels certain he has a spy embedded in her inner circle. The problem is that her pool of suspects gets deeper every day. Can Cassidy get to the bottom of what's eating away at her peaceful island home? Will voters turn out despite the outbreak of illness plaguing their tranquil town? And the even bigger question: Has darkness come to stay on Lantern Beach?

Plan of Action

A missing Navy SEAL. Danger at the boiling point. The ultimate showdown. When Police Chief Cassidy Chambers' husband, Ty, disappears, her world is turned upside down. His truck is discovered with blood inside, crashed in a ditch on Lantern Beach, but he's nowhere to be found. As they launch a manhunt to find him, Cassidy discovers that someone on the island has a deadly obsession with Ty. Meanwhile, Gilead's Cove seems to be imploding. As danger heightens, federal law enforcement officials are called in. The cult's growing threat could lead to the pinnacle standoff of good versus evil. A clear plan of action is needed or the results will be devastating. Will Cassidy find Ty in time, or will she face a gut-wrenching loss? Will Anthony Gilead finally be unmasked for who he really is and be brought to justice? Hundreds of innocent lives are at stake . . . and not everyone will come out alive.

LANTERN BEACH BLACKOUT

Dark Water

Colton Locke can't forget the black op that went terribly wrong. Desperate for a new start, he moves to Lantern Beach, North Carolina, and forms Blackout, a private security firm. Despite his hero status, he can't erase the mistakes he's made. For the past year, Elise Oliver hasn't been able to shake the feeling that there's more to her husband's death than she was told. When she finds a hidden box of his personal possessions, more questions—and suspicions—arise. The only person she trusts to help her is her husband's best friend, Colton Locke. Someone wants Elise dead. Is it because she knows too much? Or is it to keep her from finding the truth? The Blackout team must uncover dark secrets hiding beneath seemingly still waters. But those very secrets might just tear the team apart.

Safe Harbor

Guilt over past mistakes haunts former Navy SEAL Dez Rodriguez. When he's asked to guard a pop star during a music festival on Lantern Beach, he's all set for what he hopes is a breezy assignment. Bree hasn't found fame to be nearly as fulfilling as she dreamed. Instead, she's more like a carefully crafted character living out a pre-scripted story. When a stalker's threats become deadly, her life—and career—are turned upside down. From the start, Bree sees her temporary bodyguard as a player, and Dez sees Bree as a spoiled rich girl. But when they're thrown together in a fight for survival, both must learn to trust. Can Dez protect Bree—and his carefully guarded heart? Or will their safe harbor ultimately become their death trap?

Ripple Effect

Griff McIntyre never expected his ex-wife and three-year-old daughter to come to Lantern Beach. After an abduction attempt, they're desperate for safety. Now Griff's not letting either of them out of his sight. Bethany knows Griff is the only one who can protect them, despite the fact that he broke her heart. But she'll do anything to keep her daughter safe—even if it means playing nicely with a man she can't stand. As peril ripples through their lives, Griff and Bethany must work together to protect their daughter. But an unseen enemy wants something from them . . . and will stop at nothing to get it. When disaster strikes, can Griff keep his family safe? Or will past mistakes bring the ultimate failure?

Rising Tide

Benjamin James knows there's a traitor within his former command. The rest of his team might even think it's him. As danger closes in, he must clear himself and stop a deadly plot by a dangerous terrorist group. All CJ Compton wanted was a new start after her career ended under suspicion. Working as the house manager for private security group

Blackout seems perfect. But there's more trouble here than what she left behind. As the tide rushes in, the stakes continue to rise. If the Blackout team fails, it's not just Lantern Beach at stake—it's the whole country. Can Benjamin and CJ overcome their differences and work together to find the truth?

LANTERN BEACH BLACKOUT: THE NEW RECRUITS

Rocco

Former Navy SEAL and new Blackout recruit Rocco Foster is on a simple in and out mission. But the operation turns complicated when an unsuspecting woman wanders into the line of fire. Peyton Ellison's life mission is to sprinkle happiness on those around her. When a cupcake delivery turns into a fight for survival, she must trust her rescuer—a handsome stranger—to keep her safe. Rocco is determined to figure out why someone is targeting Peyton. First, he must keep the intriguing woman safe and earn her trust. But threats continue to pummel them as incriminating evidence emerges and pits them against each other. With time running out, the two must set aside both their growing attraction and their doubts about each other in order to work together. But the perilous facts they discover leave them wondering what exactly the truth is . . . and if the truth can be trusted.

Axel

Women are missing. Private security firm Blackout must find them before another victim disappears. Axel Hendrix likes to live on the edge. That's why being a Navy SEAL suited him so well. But after his last mission, he cut his losses and joined Blackout instead. His team's latest case involves an undercover investigation on Lantern Beach. Olivia Rollins came to the island to escape her problems—and danger. When trouble from her past shows up in town, she impulsively blurts she's engaged to Axel, the womanizing man she's seen while waitressing. Now, she may not be the only one in danger. So could Axel. Axel knows Olivia might be his chance to find answers and that acting like her fiancé is the perfect cover for his latest assignment. But he doesn't like throwing Olivia into the middle of such a dangerous situation. Nor is he comfortable with the feelings she stirs inside him. With Olivia's life—as well as both their hearts—on the line, Axel must uncover the truth and stop an evil plan before more lives are destroyed.

Beckett

When the daughter of a federal judge is abducted, private security firm Blackout must find her. Psychologist Samantha Reynolds doesn't know why someone is targeting her. Even after a risky mission to save her, danger still lingers. She's determined to use her insights into the human mind to help decode the deadly clues being left in the wake of her rescue. Former Navy SEAL Beckett Jones needs to figure out who's responsible for the crimes hounding Sami. He's not sure why he's so protective of the woman he rescued, but he'll do anything to keep her safe—even if it means risking his heart. As the body count rises, there's no room for error. Beckett and Sami must both tear down the careful walls they've built around themselves in order to survive. If they don't figure out who's responsible, the madman will continue his death spree . . . and one of them might be next.

Gabe

When former Navy SEAL and current Blackout operative Gabe Michaels is almost killed in a hit-and-run, the aftermath completely upends his life. He's no longer safe—and he's not the only one. Dr. Autumn Spenser came to Lantern Beach to start fresh. But while treating Gabe after his accident, she senses there's more to what happened to him than meets the eye. When she digs deeper into his past, she never expects to be drawn into a deadly dilemma. Gabe has been infatuated with the pretty doctor since the day they met. Now, can he keep her from harm? Could someone out of his league ever return his feelings or will her past hurts keep them apart? As danger continues to pummel them, Gabe and Autumn are thrown together in a quest to find answers. More important than their growing attraction, they must stay alive long enough to stop the person desperate to destroy them.

LANTERN BEACH BLACKOUT: DANGER RISING

Brandon

Physically he's protecting her. But emotionally she's never felt more exposed. The last person tech heiress Finley Cooper ever wanted to see again was Brandon Hale. Two years ago, Brandon shattered her heart. Now Finley needs protection, and, against her wishes, Brandon is assigned the job. Even worse, they must pretend to be a couple in order to find answers. Brandon, a former Navy SEAL, met Finley while on an undercover assignment in Ecuador. But he broke her trust, and now he doesn't blame Finley for hating him. As a new Blackout operative, Brandon's first assignment throws him into Finley's life 24/7. Someone wants her dead, and it's clear this person won't stop until that mission is accomplished. To keep her safe, Brandon must regain Finley's trust. Can he convince her she's more than a job to him? Or will peril permanently silence them?

Dylan

His job is to protect her. The trouble is . . . she doesn't want protection. Former Navy SEAL Dylan Granger's new assignment requires him to use both his tactical abilities and his acting skills. Hired by Katie Logan's father, his job is to protect the gutsy university professor while concealing his identity. To maintain his cover, he takes the unassuming role of her new assistant. Katie—a disgraced reporter—has stumbled upon a lead she can't ignore. Now it's clear someone is targeting her, but she refuses to back down. Her handsome new assistant is a welcome distraction from the chaos. But Dylan's skillset goes way beyond his job description, and Katie begins to suspect there's more to Dylan than he's letting on. Dylan's mission can't be disclosed—not if he wants to keep Katie safe. But as his feelings for her grow and the danger increases, keeping his secret becomes more of a challenge than he ever imagined. With innocent lives on the line, Dylan must choose between protecting Katie or savings others.

LANTERN BEACH MAYDAY

Run Aground

A dead captain on a luxury yacht leads to a tumultuous seafaring journey . . . Med student Kenzie Anderson, tired of letting others chart her future, accepts a job as second steward aboard *Almost Paradise*. But when she finds the captain dead before the charter even begins, her plans seem to capsize. Jimmy James Gamble senses something vulnerable and slightly naive about Kenzie when he finds her on the docks. Realizing danger may still be lingering close, he uses his hidden skills to earn a place on the charter. But being there causes him to risk everything —especially as more suspicious incidents occur. As they set out to sea, Kenzie and Jimmy James both wonder if they're in over their heads. They must figure out how to stop a killer before anyone onboard is hurt . . . otherwise, both their futures might just run aground.

Dead Reckoning

A yachtie fears for her life when she's the only witness to a murder . . . Kenzie Anderson knows what she saw at the harbor—a woman strangled and pushed overboard. But there's no proof of a crime . . . only her word. Jimmy James Gamble believes Kenzie, even if no one else does. As he senses the danger in the air, all he wants is to keep her away from any more trouble—especially after their last charter. Either Kenzie or the yacht they're working on seem to be a magnet for murder and mayhem. Someone is willing to kill to get what he wants—and will do so again if necessary. Can Jimmy James and Kenzie navigate these unfamiliar waters? Or will relying on dead reckoning lead them to their deaths?

Tipping Point

Awakening in a boat surrounded by nothing but water, a yachtie has no doubt someone wants her dead. Kenzie Anderson is determined not to let anyone scare her away from completing the charter season—even with the threats on her life. The only person she can trust is Captain Jimmy James Gamble, despite their tumultuous relationship. Kenzie and Jimmy James both suspect turbulent currents rush beneath the tranquil surface aboard the luxury yacht *Almost Paradise*. Secrets seem to abound, each one increasing the tension aboard the boat. As answers rise to the surface, neither Kenzie nor Jimmy James is prepared for what they find. Have they both reached their tipping points? Their adversaries want nothing more than to make Kenzie disappear . . . forever. It may be too late for a mayday call.

COMPLETE BOOK LIST

Squeaky Clean Mysteries:

    #1 Hazardous Duty

    #2 Suspicious Minds

    #2.5 It Came Upon a Midnight Crime (novella)

    #3 Organized Grime

    #4 Dirty Deeds

    #5 The Scum of All Fears

    #6 To Love, Honor and Perish

    #7 Mucky Streak

    #8 Foul Play

    #9 Broom & Gloom

    #10 Dust and Obey

    #11 Thrill Squeaker

    #11.5 Swept Away (novella)

    #12 Cunning Attractions

    #13 Cold Case: Clean Getaway

#14 Cold Case: Clean Sweep

#15 Cold Case: Clean Break

#16 Cleans to an End

While You Were Sweeping, A Riley Thomas Spinoff

The Sierra Files:

#1 Pounced

#2 Hunted

#3 Pranced

#4 Rattled

The Gabby St. Claire Diaries (a Tween Mystery series):

The Curtain Call Caper

The Disappearing Dog Dilemma

The Bungled Bike Burglaries

The Worst Detective Ever

#1 Ready to Fumble

#2 Reign of Error

#3 Safety in Blunders

#4 Join the Flub

#5 Blooper Freak

#6 Flaw Abiding Citizen

#7 Gaffe Out Loud

#8 Joke and Dagger

#9 Wreck the Halls

#10 Glitch and Famous

Raven Remington

Relentless

Holly Anna Paladin Mysteries:

#1 Random Acts of Murder

#2 Random Acts of Deceit

#2.5 Random Acts of Scrooge

#3 Random Acts of Malice

#4 Random Acts of Greed

#5 Random Acts of Fraud

#6 Random Acts of Outrage

#7 Random Acts of Iniquity

Lantern Beach Mysteries

#1 Hidden Currents

#2 Flood Watch

#3 Storm Surge

#4 Dangerous Waters

#5 Perilous Riptide

#6 Deadly Undertow

Lantern Beach Romantic Suspense

Tides of Deception

Shadow of Intrigue

Storm of Doubt

Winds of Danger

Rains of Remorse

Torrents of Fear

Lantern Beach P.D.

On the Lookout

Attempt to Locate

First Degree Murder

Dead on Arrival

Plan of Action

Lantern Beach Escape

Afterglow (a novelette)

Lantern Beach Blackout

Dark Water

Safe Harbor

Ripple Effect

Rising Tide

Lantern Beach Guardians

Hide and Seek

Shock and Awe

Safe and Sound

Lantern Beach Blackout: The New Recruits

Rocco

Axel

Beckett

Gabe

Lantern Beach Mayday

Run Aground

Dead Reckoning

Tipping Point

Lantern Beach Blackout: Danger Rising

Brandon

Dylan

Maddox

Titus

Lantern Beach Christmas

Silent Night

Crime á la Mode

Dead Man's Float

Milkshake Up

Bomb Pop Threat

Banana Split Personalities

Beach Bound Books and Beans Mysteries

Bound by Murder

Bound by Disaster

Bound by Mystery

Vanishing Ranch

Forgotten Secrets

Necessary Risk

Risky Ambition

Deadly Intent

Lethal Betrayal (coming soon)

The Sidekick's Survival Guide

The Art of Eavesdropping

The Perks of Meddling

The Exercise of Interfering

The Practice of Prying

The Skill of Snooping

The Craft of Being Covert

Saltwater Cowboys

Saltwater Cowboy

Breakwater Protector

Cape Corral Keeper

Seagrass Secrets

Driftwood Danger

Unwavering Security

Beach House Mysteries

The Cottage on Ghost Lane

The Inn on Hanging Hill

The House on Dagger Point

School of Hard Rocks Mysteries

The Treble with Murder

Crime Strikes a Chord

Tone Death

Carolina Moon Series

Home Before Dark

Gone By Dark

Wait Until Dark

Light the Dark

Taken By Dark

Suburban Sleuth Mysteries:

Death of the Couch Potato's Wife

Fog Lake Suspense:

Edge of Peril

Margin of Error

Brink of Danger

Line of Duty

Legacy of Lies

Secrets of Shame

Refuge of Redemption

Cape Thomas Series:

Dubiosity

Disillusioned

Distorted

Standalone Romantic Mystery:

The Good Girl

Suspense:

Imperfect

The Wrecking

Sweet Christmas Novella:

Home to Chestnut Grove

Standalone Romantic-Suspense:

Keeping Guard

The Last Target

Race Against Time

Ricochet

Key Witness

Lifeline

High-Stakes Holiday Reunion

Desperate Measures

Hidden Agenda

Mountain Hideaway

Dark Harbor

Shadow of Suspicion

The Baby Assignment

The Cradle Conspiracy

Trained to Defend

Mountain Survival

Dangerous Mountain Rescue

Nonfiction:

Characters in the Kitchen

Changed: True Stories of Finding God through Christian Music (out of print)

The Novel in Me: The Beginner's Guide to Writing and Publishing a Novel (out of print)

ABOUT THE AUTHOR

USA Today has called Christy Barritt's books "scary, funny, passionate, and quirky."

Christy writes both mystery and romantic suspense novels that are clean with underlying messages of faith. Her books have sold more than three million copies and have won the Daphne du Maurier Award for Excellence in Suspense and Mystery, have been twice nominated for the Romantic Times Reviewers' Choice Award, and have finaled for both a Carol Award and Foreword Magazine's Book of the Year.

She is married to her Prince Charming, a man who thinks she's hilarious—but only when she's not trying to be. Christy is a self-proclaimed klutz, an avid music lover who's known for spontaneously bursting into song, and a road trip aficionado.

When she's not working or spending time with her family, she enjoys singing, playing the guitar, and exploring small, unsuspecting towns where people have no idea how accident-prone she is.

Find Christy online at:
www.christybarritt.com
www.facebook.com/christybarritt
www.twitter.com/cbarritt

Sign up for Christy's newsletter to get information on all of her latest releases here: **www.christybarritt.com/newsletter-sign-up/**